Isaiah glanced up, and Adelaide waved. He headed straight toward her, whistling a tune.

As he neared she couldn't help noticing how attractive he was and admitted to herself how much she loved his easygoing demeanor—so unlike her dad or Harold. His tawny hair glistened in the late afternoon sun, and when he stopped next to her, she caught a hint of the musky scent that was becoming familiar.

"Glad to ▮▮▮▮▮▮▮▮▮▮▮▮▮▮▮▮▮" He grabbed a couple of ▮▮▮▮▮▮▮▮▮▮▮▮▮▮▮d toward her apartment. S▮▮▮▮▮▮▮▮▮▮▮▮▮▮▮red him.

"Where do ▮▮▮▮▮▮▮▮▮▮▮▮▮▮▮

"I have ther▮▮▮▮▮▮▮▮▮▮ room."

"Should have known." He grinned at her and set the boxes on the coffee table. "How about if I carry them in and set them here? You can take them to the appropriate spot."

Adelaide nodded her agreement, appreciating his care in keeping appearances appropriate. Even earlier, he had hovered in the doorway.

In no time the Rodeo sat empty. "You must have stored everything in Texas," he commented. "You sure travel light for a woman. All the girls I see moving into the dorms have twice as many boxes."

She nodded, letting him think whatever he wanted. She didn't intend to explain this was all she owned in the entire world.

JERI ODELL is a native of Tucson, Arizona. She has been married almost thirty-seven years and has three wonderful adult children and three precious grandchildren. Jeri holds family dear to her heart, second only to God. This is Jeri's eighth novel for Heartsong. She has also written eight novellas, a nonfiction book, and articles on family issues for several Christian publications. She thanks God for the privilege of writing for Him. When not writing or reading, she is busy in her church teaching on marriage and parenting. If you'd like, you can e-mail her at Jeri.Odell@gmail.com.

Books by Jeri Odell

Don't miss out on any of our super romances. Write to us at the following address for information on our newest releases and club information.

Heartsong Presents Readers' Service
PO Box 721
Uhrichsville, OH 44683

Or visit www.heartsongpresents.com

Perfect Ways

Jeri Odell

Heartsong Presents

This book is dedicated to my friend Monica, who has never failed to point me to the Lord in hard times and times of distress. May He bless you tenfold, my dear friend.

A note from the Author:
I love to hear from my readers! You may correspond with me by writing:

Jeri Odell
Author Relations
PO Box 721
Uhrichsville, OH 44683

ISBN 978-1-60260-885-6

PERFECT WAYS

Our mission is to publish and distribute inspirational products offering exceptional value and biblical encouragement to the masses.

PRINTED IN THE U.S.A.

one

"Summer has ended," Adelaide English stated matter-of-factly to her daughter, Lissa. But truth be told, her entire life as she knew it had ended as well. They loaded the last box into the back of the hunter green Isuzu Rodeo. Never could she have imagined trading her Volvo sedan for an SUV, but she needed the extra room it afforded to move across country. "Who'd have guessed a year ago that my every belonging would fit into one vehicle?" She tried to keep the pain and bitterness out of her voice, but fell short.

"I'm sorry, Mom." Lissa wrapped an arm around her mother's shoulders, giving her a tight squeeze. "Daddy didn't mean for this to happen."

Adelaide looked at the huge Tudor-style home she'd been forced to sell. Tears pooled in her eyes. Resentment lodged itself in her throat. "No, he didn't." *But it doesn't change the ugly facts.* She didn't voice her thoughts, not wanting Lissa to feel all the horrible things she did toward Harold. Some people you really didn't know until they died—at least that was the case with her late husband. So many secrets.

"Mom, three years ago when I left home for my freshman year of college, do you remember what you said?"

"I'm not sure. In regard to what?"

"You told me how much you wished you'd gone to college instead of marrying Daddy so quickly. Now is your chance. You got to be Daddy's wife for twenty-five years, and forty-five is by no means too old to finish college. So go—chase your dream. God's giving you a second chance."

A second chance? Was that what this was? It sure didn't feel like anything as wonderful as a second chance. It felt like the end of everything. The end of home and family and all she held dear. *Stop with the drama—I'm pathetic!* Adelaide lifted her chin and sucked in a deep breath. College was her dream when she had the big house. Now she wasn't so sure.

She hugged Lissa tight, not wanting to let go. The big, empty house lurking in the background reminded her of how different her life was now. Not only forced to sell the house, but in the past fourteen months, she'd sold their furnishings, their expensive vehicles, and even most of her jewelry to pay off the enormous debts Harold had accrued gambling. It was his hideous secret that no longer remained undisclosed.

Enough money remained to cover Lissa's senior year at Wheaton and to get Adelaide to Idaho and pay for her first semester at the Lord's College. *Please, God, let me get that resident director's position,* she asked for about the hundredth time. It would provide a free place to live and help cover her expenses.

Lissa pulled out of the long hug. "I love you, Mom, and I'm proud of you. It takes guts to do what you're doing."

"Either that or complete insanity." Adelaide winked, not wanting their last moments together to be eclipsed by sorrow. She stroked her daughter's silky ash-blond hair, the same shade Harold's had been. "This is it, kiddo. I love you, and I'll see you at Christmas."

"Maybe Thanksgiving—if I get a decent job. And we'll text or talk every day."

Adelaide placed one last kiss on Lissa's cheek. They headed for their respective cars. Adelaide followed her daughter's Honda Civic out of the circle driveway and through the neighborhood. The upscale Dallas area had been home to both of them for two decades—all but a few months of Lissa's life. She knew no other home. Now with God's help, they'd both find a new and better life. If only the pit of her stomach believed that.

At the stop sign, Lissa stuck her arm out the window and waved one last time. She took a right, heading toward I-75 and her senior year at Wheaton. She'd spend the night with her roommate in Joplin, Missouri, and then they'd drive on together. Adelaide waited until the little blue car disappeared from sight, thankful her daughter didn't have to make the whole fifteen-hour drive alone or in one day.

Adelaide took a left and made her way to 114 West, driving toward her future in Coeur d'Alene, Idaho, at the Lord's College. With two long days of travel ahead of her, she'd stop in Denver tonight and finish her nearly two-thousand-mile trek tomorrow.

"Summer's over and so is my pity party," Adelaide stated in the rearview mirror at the next traffic light. *Lord, this is a second chance, so as I start this new season of my life, give me a hope and a future. Turn my mourning into dancing.* Many prayers rose between Texas and Idaho.

❧

Isaiah Shepherd crossed the lush grass toward the administration building. He always avoided crowded sidewalks, even though today few wandered the campus. He liked the feel of God's earth beneath his feet.

He felt the same excitement that he did every year as the first day of school approached. He relished teaching the Bible, his favorite subject, at this little Christian college. He enjoyed meeting the eager freshmen and challenging their thinking about God. Most of all, he just loved the Lord, and it was good to be alive.

Today he wore his other hat as the director of resident life. He entered the building through the rear, heading down the hall to the conference room where the interviews were scheduled. Walt and Linda Richards sat at the large table, where much college business took place. Before they were aware of his presence, he caught them in a tender moment, and a pang of longing plunged deep into his heart. He missed what they shared, but not enough to risk loving another woman, unable to bear the pain of possible loss.

"I invited Linda to join us, so the three interviewees wouldn't feel intimidated by an all-male panel. Is that okay by you?" Walt Richards asked. That was the thing Isaiah liked most about his boss and close friend—Walt always considered ways to make others more comfortable and less intimidated.

"Great idea," Isaiah said, smiling at Walt and Linda. She'd taken the job of Walt's administrative assistant a few years back when their nest emptied.

"Where's James?" Isaiah asked, expecting to see the third member of their panel.

"Right here," he said, walking through the door. "Any concerns before we get started?"

"Nope. You?" He instinctively knew James wouldn't like Adelaide English, but she was his preference. They all settled around the table with résumés and applications laid out in front of them.

"I'll let you know when we're finished." James took his seat at the head of the table. "I do have some uneasiness about Adelaide English, but am not ready to voice my apprehensions yet. Some things don't show up on paper but glare at you when you're face-to-face." He flipped her application over. "Is Ms. English our first interview?"

"She is," Linda said, checking the schedule. "I'll see if she's here."

A moment later Linda reentered the room with a forty-something woman wearing a pale pink silk blouse, white linen skirt, and pearls. But what drew Isaiah's attention was her understated beauty. And man was she ever beautiful—in a classic, unpretentious sort of way. He, James, and Walt rose, and he pulled out the chair to his right. "Ms. English." He nodded toward the empty seat.

She took the chair and smiled—a stiff, forced effort—appearing as uncomfortable as a snowman at the beach. Her hair reminded him of the cup of rich dark coffee he'd had in place of breakfast just thirty minutes before. It was styled to perfection in a sort of layered, semicurled, windblown look. Her eyes—large, luminous pools the same shade as her hair—met his, her expression tentative.

In those eyes he saw the most forlorn look he'd seen in years. She appeared more frightened than any freshman he'd come across. It was more than that, though. A look of pain, hurt, or possibly betrayal lingered in their depths. What had happened to wound her soul?

She squirmed under his inquiring gaze and broke eye contact. It was as if God had given him some sort of insight because he knew something tormented her. Quite honestly, she probably packed a truckload of baggage and maybe even a million problems he didn't need, but he knew immediately she was the one he wanted to hire. Julie used to tease him about championing the underdog. Maybe it was true.

He cleared his throat. "I'm Isaiah Shepherd, the director of resident life; and this is James Dunlap, vice president of college affairs; Walt Richards, vice president of student affairs; and Linda Richards, Walt's wife and secretary."

"Nice to meet y'all." She had the sweet sound of Texas in her voice, and it made her all the more appealing.

"Adelaide English, everyone." They all took their seats.

"I noticed from your résumé you haven't worked in twenty-one years." James jumped right in, heading for the jugular.

Her face darkened to a red hue. "No, I haven't. That's when my daughter was born," she stated apologetically.

"And we commend your decision to stay at home with your daughter," Walt assured her. "Linda and I made the same choice for our children." He shot a disapproving glare in James's direction.

James coughed, and all eyes returned to him. "What do you feel you can offer the resident assistants if you get the director's position?" He apparently wanted to get the interview over with. No warm, fuzzy, get-to-know-you questions.

She fidgeted a moment before taking a deep breath and looking directly into Isaiah's eyes. He swallowed hard. Then she faced James, raising her chin a fraction. "I have a college-aged daughter, so I understand the needs, hopes, and fears of a young woman in her late teens and early twenties. I hope to offer them friendship, guidance, and a touch of mothering."

"Mothering is the last thing most of these girls want." James spoke more bluntly than usual. "Having ten RAs under your direction is a bit different from raising one daughter, don't you think? Do you have any managerial skills?"

Both Isaiah and Walt had given Ms. English high marks on her application. James seemed to want to make certain they all saw her glaring inability.

She glanced down at her lap before answering; then she raised her chin and looked James straight in the eye. "I've managed a household for two decades. I know I can do this, if you'll give me a chance." A note of desperation found its way into her tone. "I really need this job." She swallowed hard.

"Adelaide." Linda reached across the table and patted her hand. "Tell us about your faith walk." She shot James a glare that said, *Enough.*

At this question, her features relaxed. "My mom took me and my two younger brothers to church every Sunday. I asked Jesus into my heart as a young girl, but made a lordship commitment about five years ago."

"And by lordship commitment, you mean what, exactly?" James asked.

"I gave Him not just my heart, but my life." Now confidence radiated from her.

"What would your spiritual goals be as an RD?" Walt asked.

"I'd like to encourage the girls in their walks with God. Have a weekly Bible study and prayer time. Assign them prayer and accountability partners. I thought once a month I'd plan a social event for us."

"These are busy college students," James injected. "Sometimes those type of activities happen at midnight. Can you keep up with that sort of schedule?"

She heard the *at your age* in his question. "I hope to." She shrugged.

"Do you mind if we ask you a few personal questions? You are free to choose not to answer, but as a Christian organization, we need to know your family situation." Walt's smile encouraged trust.

Isaiah hoped her answers would highlight the fact that she was the right candidate for the job. But maybe it was better if she didn't get it. Could he afford to have her around, reminding him he grew lonelier all the time? She was the first woman he'd found attractive since Julie died nearly a decade ago.

Besides, in his estimation, she might lack the self-confidence necessary to relate well to college kids. But somehow he believed her to be God's choice for the job anyway.

&

The moment Adelaide dreaded had arrived. Certain Dr. Dunlap already disliked her, she thought this ought to frost the cake for him. "Go ahead." She hoped those words sounded calmer than she felt. *Lord, please don't make me share about Harold's gambling or how broke I am.*

"You have a daughter, but you haven't mentioned a husband. Are you recently divorced?" Dr. Dunlap asked. Sitting at the head of the table in his three-piece suit caused him to appear even more formidable.

"I was widowed fourteen months ago. I've dreamed of attending a Christian college since I was ten. Now seems like the right time."

Linda smiled at her. Her blue eyes filled with compassion. "Where's your daughter living?"

"She's starting her senior year at Wheaton in a couple of weeks, and she went back early to settle in and get a job."

"And how did you end up here? It's a long way from Texas," Dr. Shepherd asked. He looked the most casual of the interviewers in his blue denim shirt and jeans. His smile revealed deep creases in his rugged face.

"My cousin attended this college when I was a little girl. I dreamed of coming here, too, only my family couldn't afford to send me. I never considered any other university." She felt silly verbalizing her childhood dream.

"Well, we're glad you're here," Linda said.

"Thank you."

"Do you understand the responsibilities of a resident director?" Dr. Dunlap asked.

"I believe so." Adelaide knew she wasn't going to get the job, so why did it even matter?

Dr. Shepherd faced her. "You'll have ten assistants under you, and they'll each have fifteen or so students in their wing of the dorm." His eyes were warm, kind.

"You're ultimately responsible for the one hundred and fifty or so girls who reside in Zion Hall. Their parents count on us to direct them and watch over them. It's a huge task, Mrs. English." Dr. Dunlap seemed determined that everyone realize how incapable she was for this awesome duty.

"I understand." *Maybe I'm too far out of my league. Maybe this is God's way of showing me I can't rise to the occasion.*

"Do you have any questions for us?" Dr. Richards asked. He seemed the most compassionate of the three men sitting around the table.

"No. Thank you for your time." Adelaide rose to leave, certain she needed to get out of there before the lump in her throat burst and an overabundance of tears poured forth.

Dr. Shepherd rose as well and walked her to the door. "I'll get back to you in the next few days."

She nodded. *Why bother?* The outcome was obvious.

Once she was outside, the tears fell. Since Harold's death, she'd cried more than she had in the entire forty-four previous years. She drove back to the dingy little hotel room through a haze of remorse. *What now, God?* If only she knew.

Walking by faith proved much harder when hope disappeared and plans failed. She pulled into Starbucks. After a Mocha Frap and a conversation with Lissa, she'd feel so much better. Hey, Starbucks—she could get a job at Starbucks. Sure. Why not? Dr. James Dunlap might be able to take the job from her, but he couldn't steal the dream. Nope, the dream was all hers.

two

"Welcome." Linda threw open the front door of their home for Isaiah to enter. "Dinner's almost ready. James just got here. He's out back with Walt trying to get him to take the steaks off the grill before they burn, but you know Walt; well done is the only way he grills."

Isaiah chuckled, remembering the countless rubbery, over-cooked steaks he'd eaten here. Thank heaven the company was always better than the food. "I'll make my way out there, unless you need help in the kitchen?"

"No, you go salvage the steaks. I'll be out in a few minutes with the salad and baked potatoes."

The minute Isaiah stepped through the sliding glass door, Walt said, "Zay, buddy, explain to James that I do know when to remove the meat from the fire."

"I'm staying out of this one, but those do look more than ready," he commented upon closer inspection.

Within minutes the four of them sat under the umbrella table, and Walt blessed the food. "Amen," Isaiah echoed after the prayer. He drew in a deep breath of clean Idaho air. "Why would anyone want crowded cities over small towns, buildings over glorious views of God's creation—"

"And cement over dirt," Walt finished for him. Everyone laughed.

"Exactly." His eyes roamed over the Spokane River just past their deck and down the steep incline. Man, he loved this state and felt so thankful to the Lord he'd moved here with Julie shortly after college.

"Let's get down to our decision," James suggested, never one to waste time on small talk if business was at hand.

"I think Adelaide English is the best choice for the job, but more important, I think she's God's choice." Isaiah sawed through his T-bone with a steak knife.

"I disagree," James interjected, then took a bite of his garlic bread.

Her sad, deep brown eyes came to mind, and a part of Isaiah longed to see them aglow with happiness—the insane part. *I'm not falling for anyone ever again*, he reminded his traitorous thoughts.

"Why?" Walt asked, sounding a bit defensive. "I really liked her."

"It has nothing to do with liking her. She's not right for the job—too old, too uptight, too irrelevant."

"I think her age is a real plus." Isaiah reached for his iced tea. "Tell me what Miss Andrews or Miss Lindsay can offer that Mrs. English can't."

"Miss Andrews is a business major. She's taken management courses."

"And she's a ditsy blonde," Walt insisted. "She may be a business major, but I don't see her as the strongest candidate. I observed no leadership skills."

"Walt's right. A class in management doesn't make someone a leader." Why was he fighting for her? He knew she'd only bring him trouble on a personal level. He'd thought about her several times since yesterday. He just didn't need her around as a reminder of what he'd never let himself have again. Good thing the school had a strict policy against staff dating students or other staff members.

"Well, she was captain of her cheerleading squad in high

school," Walt chided, glancing up from her application. "Maybe that makes her a solid leader."

"Miss Lindsay has been in student government the past three years," Isaiah said.

"I'd choose either of these girls over Mrs. English." James usually took their kidding in stride, but this evening he seemed perturbed.

"Yes, and Miss Lindsay is more qualified than Miss Andrews, but I don't think she's the best choice for the job," Isaiah stated, not letting James's higher position sway him.

"What makes Mrs. English the best choice?" James asked.

"Not only does her age make her more mature and settled, but the skills she's gained running a household clinch it for me. I've watched my wife all these years." Walt sent Linda a smile filled with admiration. "Tremendous organizational and managerial skills are required."

"I feel like she'd nurture the girls. In my mind, that's a real plus," Isaiah said. "Worth more than management skills. And she has some spiritual depth."

"Mrs. English has less education than the other two applicants. Technically, our guidelines state that an RD must be a senior or above. She only completed her sophomore year, and that was ages ago." James wiped his mouth with his napkin. He wasn't giving in on this one. "She doesn't qualify for the job. Besides that, did you see how stiff and uptight she is? The girls won't relate to her. And will they respect her if she's one of their freshman peers?"

"Oh come on," Isaiah said. "She may not have her junior year completed, but her age and life experience more than qualify her for the job. Another plus—in my mind—is the fact that she will be around another two or three years. We won't have to do this again next year. And you know as well as I do, these kids will never consider her a peer whether or not she's an RD. Her age will separate them, so in my mind, it won't be a problem."

"James, this isn't like you. What are you being so stubborn about?" Walt asked.

"It just doesn't make sense to me. Something doesn't add up." He rubbed the back of his neck. "You have this woman who comes two thousand miles to attend college. She's lived in Texas her whole life—same address for two decades. She leaves everything to come here, live in a dorm. Why? Texas is filled with Christian colleges. I don't get it."

"You left life as you knew it when your family died in that car crash," Walt reminded him quietly. "Maybe she's searching for a fresh start, just like you were when you moved up here. She really seems to need the job. Can't you give her a break?"

James sighed.

Only Walt could call someone out like that, yet not offend.

"Maybe it makes more sense than I want to admit or remember. Sometimes people do need a fresh start."

Isaiah recalled the look in her eyes. "I think she's a woman with some deep hurts. Didn't you see it in her eyes?"

"Maybe she needs to take care of herself before she can take care of others." James shook his head.

"Sometimes it's in serving others that we heal. I was pretty hurt when Julie died. It was teaching that impassioned me to move on."

"True, and let's remember, God doesn't always choose the most qualified. Sometimes He picks the least likely. Look at His motley crew of disciples if you need proof." Walt obviously wasn't about to back down.

"And look at the motley group I got saddled with." James

chuckled. "Let's spend some time in prayer about this." They moved away from the table to the lawn chairs at the other end of the deck. There they spent the next half hour or so asking God to guide them in their decision.

"Amen." James ended their prayer time. "Walt, who do you think the Lord's chosen for this job?"

"Adelaide English." His answer held no apology.

Isaiah shrugged. "I'm in agreement. James?"

"I guess we'll give Mrs. English a shot." He grinned at the others. "I just hope a few months from now we don't have a mess on our hands and you're not all apologizing to me."

Isaiah hoped for Adelaide's sake, his sake, and the sake of the school that James was wrong. That night he couldn't quit thinking about Adelaide English. He wondered what deep secrets dulled her eyes. He hoped she was only seeking a fresh start and not running from some deep pain in her past. And he hoped his heart didn't betray him. He'd not love another woman. He absolutely would not—no matter how beautiful she was.

ﾞ

Adelaide's cell phone rang the following morning—two days after the dreaded interview. She still hadn't heard from them. Her heart pounded in both anticipation and dread as THE LORD'S COLLEGE was printed across her screen. Should she answer or let them leave the "thanks but no thanks" message on her voice mail? After staring at it for several seconds, she flipped it open.

"Hello?" She hated the weak, pathetic quiver in her voice.

"Mrs. English?"

Her stomach knotted tighter upon hearing a man's voice on the other end of the line. "Yes?"

"It's Isaiah Shepherd. I'm calling about the RD position."

The one I didn't get? "Yes?"

"Could you meet me in my office in, say, an hour?"

"Yes." Why must he insist on telling her in person?

He gave her directions to his office. "Well, I'll see you then."

"Yes. Thank you. I'll be there."

Adelaide shut her phone and laid it back on the nightstand. Then she grabbed it and punched 2 with her index finger. In seconds Lissa's phone was ringing in her ear. *Oh, I hope she's not in a job interview.* Adelaide paced across the tiny room, leaning on the desk and drumming her nails against the wood.

"Lis, I'm so glad you're not busy. Dr. Shepherd called—"

"You got the job!"

"I don't know. I have to go to his office in an hour."

"I don't think he'd call you in to tell you no."

"They might. Who knows?" She shrugged. "I have no idea how these things are done nowadays. At least I don't have to face that mean Dr. Dunlap. He did not like me, not one bit."

"Mom, don't be silly. Everyone loves you."

"He didn't. Anyway, will you be praying? I don't want to fall apart when Dr. Shepherd tells me they decided on the young blond cheerleader type who was in the lobby when I left my interview."

"I will be. I love you, Mom. Remember what you always tell me. God's best isn't always what we expect. You spent my whole life telling me that, and sometimes I hated the reminder." Lissa giggled. "Since Dad died, I sometimes sound like the mom."

"You're right, of course. God will have something better for me down the road." Adelaide had said that phrase a million times throughout her life. Why did she struggle to believe it now? "I've actually got a plan B—Starbucks."

"Starbucks?"

"It's the one familiar thing in my life right now. A friendly place that looks almost exactly the same as the one back home. I spent all day yesterday there reading ads for jobs and cheap housing. I have a couple of possibilities lined up."

"Good for you, Mom."

Adelaide smiled. "I do feel rather proud of myself for not turning tail and running home. Oh yeah, there is no home to run to," she half-joked.

"Maybe that's all part of God's plan to get you to stay."

"Nowhere else to go—that's for sure. Hey, I've got a big important meeting. No time for idle chitchat."

"I've got a job interview, too, so gotta run as well. Call me tonight and tell me all about this meeting with the ominous Dr. Shepherd."

"Okay. Bye, honey. Don't forget to pray." *And he's not so ominous. He's ruggedly handsome with compassionate eyes and strong muscular arms.* Yes, to her own dismay, she'd noticed.

Adelaide then dialed her best friend in Texas. It was basically a repeat of the conversation with Lissa. Monica promised to pray as well.

On her way to Dr. Shepherd's office almost an hour later, Adelaide passed Linda in the hall. "Adelaide, it's great to see you again." Linda's blue eyes twinkled their welcome.

"Hello, Linda. It's nice to see a familiar face."

"Why don't we have lunch one day real soon? I can show you around Coeur d'Alene."

"I'd like that."

"I have a better idea. Why don't you come to church with Walt and me on Sunday?"

Adelaide glanced at her watch.

"I'm sorry. You're probably on your way to meet Zay. I'll call you, and we'll set something up," Linda promised.

"I'd love that, really. I didn't mean to be rude, but Dr. Shepherd awaits."

Linda smiled. "Not at all. His office is the next door on your right."

"Thanks. I'll speak with you soon, I hope."

Adelaide paused before going in. She straightened her linen blazer and brushed at the wrinkles in the matching peach-colored skirt. Upon entering, she was greeted by a friendly older lady who led her right into an inner office where Dr. Shepherd sat at a large mahogany desk. He rose when they crossed the threshold.

"Mrs. English is here, Dr. Shepherd."

"Thank you, Rose. Good morning, Mrs. English. Please make yourself comfortable." He gestured to the plush chairs facing him from across the desk. His smile appeared genuine.

Would he be this cordial if I didn't get the job?

She heard the door close behind Rose.

"Well, Adelaide. You don't mind if I call you Adelaide, do you?" His demeanor was warm and friendly.

"No, Dr. Shepherd, that will be fine." *Please just get this over with.*

"And please, call me Isaiah."

She nodded her agreement. No point arguing. She'd have no need to call him anything a few minutes from now.

"Adelaide, after much prayer, the committee would like to offer you the RD position—that is, if you're still interested?"

Were they hoping she wasn't? She felt tears of relief pooling in her eyes. *Not here, Adelaide. You know it's improper to show anything but polite emotion in public, especially in front of strangers.* Harold's reprimand echoed through her head. She tried to pull herself together. She blinked a few times.

"Thank you." If he hadn't seen the emotion on her face, he surely heard it in her voice.

"If you'll excuse me for a moment, I'll be right back. I'll get the new employee forms for you to fill out." His brown eyes held compassion.

She nodded, not daring to speak. Realizing he was giving her a few minutes alone to regain her composure, she suddenly appreciated the man. After he left, she spent the next moments thanking the Lord and repenting for her lack of faith.

When Isaiah returned, Adelaide's poise was in place. He took the chair next to her rather than behind the desk. While he explained several forms, she couldn't help noticing his musky scent. She'd not been this close to a man since Harold died. And suddenly she realized Isaiah Shepherd was all man.

His striped oxford shirt was rolled up at the cuffs, exposing his tanned forearms. His jeans looked new, as did his Nikes. But what fascinated her most was the dimple lodged in his right cheek.

"Well, that about covers it. Do you have any questions?"

"I don't believe so." In studying him, she'd missed most of his instructions.

"If you do, Rose can help. I have a quick meeting down the hall, so you may use my desk to fill these out. I should be back in twenty to thirty minutes. Do you mind waiting if you're done before I get back? I'll have someone show you around campus and your new apartment."

She nodded. "I'll wait."

He grabbed some keys from the top drawer. "Go ahead and bring those over here. It'll be easier from this side." He pulled out his chair for her.

She sank into the big leather seat and felt swallowed by its enormity.

"I'll be back as soon as I can break away," he said on his way out the door.

The scent of him lingered. *What's wrong with me?*

Adelaide took a moment to examine his office. A woman's picture gazed back from a bookshelf to her left. Embarrassment flooded her. He was married. She'd been attracted to a married man. Horrified, she quickly filled out the forms, sensing the woman's blue eyes mocking her.

three

When Isaiah returned from his meeting, he found Adelaide sitting in the outer office waiting room where Rose's desk stood. "All done?" He wondered why she'd moved out there.

"Yes." She sat with spine straight, shoulders squared. *Does this woman ever relax?* On both their encounters, she seemed so uptight—the interview he could understand, but now she had the job.

"Where's Rose?" he wondered aloud.

"Oh, I'm supposed to remind you that she had a support staff meeting and would be gone the rest of the afternoon." Adelaide stood and straightened her skirt.

"I'd forgotten about that and was hoping she'd take you on the campus tour." He sighed. "That means Linda is unavailable as well. Why don't you come back tomorrow morning, and I'll arrange a tour?"

Adelaide's expression fell. "I. . .ah. . .I was hoping to move in this afternoon." For the second time, he noted desperation in her voice.

He understood her wanting to get settled. "All right." He glanced at his watch. "Do you know where Zion Hall is located?"

She shook her head.

Of course not.

"Tell you what, I'll walk you over there." He eyed her appearance. "Do you have any other shoes?" he asked, holding the door open for her. When she brushed past him, a spark

24

akin to electricity shot through him. He cleared his throat and refocused. "Those pumps aren't conducive to a walk across campus. The campus is pretty spread out, and Zion Hall is at the opposite end."

Adelaide shrugged. "This is all I have with me."

He nodded, noting he'd unintentionally embarrassed her. "Tell you what, why don't you drive back to your hotel, grab your things, and call my cell when you get back to campus. I'll give you a brief tour and the keys to your new place. You can move in this afternoon."

"Thank you." Relief washed over her features.

He gave her his cell number, and she programmed it into her phone. "See you in a bit." She moved toward a dark green Rodeo. Not the car he'd have guessed was hers.

"And Adelaide."

She stopped and turned back to face him. The large sunglasses hid most of her face.

"If you don't mind, wear something more practical."

She nodded, but the droop of her shoulders let him know he'd somehow offended her. "Lord, give me Your wisdom to tread carefully. She seems somehow fragile." Fragile, beautiful, appealing. The appealing part threw him. She wasn't his type at all; yet the attraction remained undeniable.

In about an hour his cell phone rang. Adelaide greeted him. "I'm in front of your building, but the door is locked. I'm ready whenever you are."

"Okay." He rose from his desk. "We'll give that tour a shot now." He left the building and moved toward her. She now wore a pair of navy slacks, matching print blouse, and stylish-looking sandals. He led her away from the administration building and through the grass toward a clump of trees. He remained quiet. Getting personal with her was the last thing he desired. Well, maybe he desired it, but it wasn't wise.

"Where are we going?" she questioned, glancing back at the campus he'd promised to show her.

"My favorite spot." He hadn't planned to, but he grabbed her elbow when she slipped slightly on the wet grass. He guided her down the dirt path toward the river. Catching a whiff of her perfume—something elegant and sophisticated and feminine—accentuated his loneliness.

"Where are you from?" she asked.

Figuring talking was safer than pondering, he jumped in. "Originally Wisconsin. I came west for college—to the LA area, actually. I met Julie there. We married during our senior year, moved up here after graduation, then had a couple of boys. She died ten years ago from cancer. Fought a valiant fight, but didn't make it. Here I am, and here we are." He paused at the slight decline that led down to the water below.

"I didn't realize your wife had died." Her gaze held compassion and sadness and maybe even relief. "Was that Julie's picture I saw in your office?"

Nodding, he realized they needed a change of topic. He glanced down at her impractical footwear. "I guess this is as far as we go unless you want sandals full of sand." He paused, listening to the sound of the water. "The first thing you'll have to learn, Addie, is how to dress like a college kid." Tempted to pick her up and carry her to his secluded bench, he thought better of that idea. He'd probably give this uneasy woman a heart attack right there on the spot.

"Addie?"

He'd said his new version of her name with a warmth and familiarity he hadn't intended. "Adelaide sounds so prim and proper. I like Addie. Don't you?"

"I guess, but only my closest and dearest friend calls me that. Somehow I can't picture myself as anything but Adelaide." Her brows drew together in a frown. "It's fine if you call me Addie, but I hope you don't expect me to dress like my daughter and her friends."

"No, just as comfortable as possible. And *never* in heels." He couldn't help teasing her.

She smiled and did relax a little. He could see it in her face. And man was she beautiful when she smiled.

Lifting her eyebrows, she drawled, "I thought our tour would include sidewalks. I had no idea I'd need a pair of hiking boots."

He chuckled. *So the lady has a sense of humor.* "Don't you know the best things in life are hard to come by? You never find them down sidewalks, but on mountaintops and backwoods roads."

"And in the hearts of people you love." Her voice came from a distant place.

"Exactly!" She must be referencing her husband. "And you'll never find this view or this peace anywhere near a sidewalk."

He stretched his arms out. "This is the best homework spot and quiet-time place on the planet."

"I'll remember that, and I'll chuck the heels if I ever plan to head this way again."

"You don't sound like you will." The disappointment surprised him. Why did he care? He wasn't exactly sure, but for some reason he wanted her to like this little slice of heaven as much as he did.

"Nature's not my thing. I'd much rather sit in an air-conditioned Starbucks than on some dirt patch next to a river where I'm always swatting at some pesky mosquito," she drawled in her slow Texas way, slapping her forearm to prove her point.

Another reason we'd never work. "You don't know what you're missing." He shrugged. "Then back to the concrete world of buildings and sidewalks for you, madam." He resumed his jovial attitude, glad he'd seen another glaring flaw in the idea of a *them*.

"I take it you're an outdoorsman?"

"If I had my way, I'd teach outside and occasionally do. When spring fever hits, I drag my students to the amphitheater. Lucky for you, I don't do that much in the fall."

"Why lucky for me?" Her brow furrowed.

"You're in my OT class. Haven't you looked at your schedule?"

"I've been so worried about this job that I haven't. At least not closely. Besides, the professors are all meaningless names to me at this point."

"Well, one of those meaningless names is mine," he teased. "Every Monday, Wednesday, and Friday at eight thirty in the morning, this meaningless name will lecture you about the Old Testament."

"I didn't realize you taught."

"I do. It's the best part of working here. Well, here we are, Miss Adelaide, back to sidewalks and buildings."

"This is a beautiful campus. So green, with grass and trees in abundance. It looks quite old."

"It is. Much of it was built in the early 1900s."

He pointed out all the buildings as they passed. She paid attention and repeated each name he recited. "And this is Zion Hall." They stopped in front of the imposing three-story brick building. "Come on. I'll show you your new home." He unlocked the door and led her through the empty lobby to her front door. "The students begin arriving next week."

A small white board hung beside her door. It said WELCOME, NEW RD. He picked up the dry erase marker dangling from a string next to it and wrote ADDIE'S PLACE. He unlocked the dead bolt, stood aside for her to enter, and lingered in the doorway.

A smile lit her face, and relief rushed through him. "It's very cute."

"I know it's small."

"Yes, but the wicker furniture gives it an airy feel." He waited near the door while she wandered through all four tiny rooms.

"It's a palace compared to the hotel I've been holed up in. Thank you for giving me this job. I know the committee, or at least Dr. Dunlap, had reservations, but I won't let you down."

"I'm not concerned that you will. Relax and enjoy the experience. There is nothing like college kids to keep you young. Now, let's head back and get your stuff."

Isaiah pondered the woman next to him on the walk back to the admin building. Adelaide—a tall, beautiful woman with her soft, smooth-as-silk, and definitely Southern voice—intrigued him more than he cared to admit. He guessed that she'd been trained to be prim and proper; it seemed there was no room in her life for emotion or embarrassment. In his viewpoint, she lived in a self-imposed prison.

Suddenly he wanted to be the one to show her the freedom the Lord had shown him—freedom to be himself. He longed to teach her all about her worth in Christ and God's wonderful outdoors and help her find success in college life. If only she'd let him. . . *No! What am I thinking? Getting close to her, investing in her, would not only put my heart at risk, but would break the rules set by the college.*

❧

Later that afternoon Adelaide parked her Rodeo in front of Zion Hall. She searched her purse for the keys Isaiah had given her and tried to remember which did what. After three tries she got the heavy glass door open. A few more tries and her apartment was unlocked, too. She'd just propped the glass door open with a box from the back of her SUV when she spotted Isaiah avoiding sidewalks, tromping through the grass, heading toward her building. She smiled, liking how sure of himself he was.

Watching him, her heart quickened. *Addie*—his nickname for her floated through her memory again. The way he said it—tender, yet reverent, almost like an endearment—touched her very core. *This is crazy! I'm a grown woman acting like a silly schoolgirl.* But at least she felt better about her foolish crush after realizing he wasn't a married man, but a widower.

Isaiah glanced up, and Adelaide waved. He headed straight toward her, whistling a tune. As he neared she couldn't help noticing how attractive he was and admitted to herself how much she loved his easygoing demeanor—so unlike her dad or Harold. His tawny hair glistened in the late afternoon sun, and when he stopped next to her, she caught a hint of the musky scent that was becoming familiar.

"Glad to see that you haven't unloaded yet." He grabbed a couple of boxes out of the Rodeo and headed toward her apartment. She picked up another one and followed him.

"Where do you want these?"

"I have them labeled with the correct room."

"Should have known." He grinned at her and set the boxes on the coffee table. "How about if I carry them in and set them here? You can take them to the appropriate spot."

Adelaide nodded her agreement, appreciating his care in keeping appearances appropriate. Even earlier, he had hovered in the doorway.

In no time the Rodeo sat empty. "You must have stored everything in Texas," he commented. "You sure travel light for a woman. All the girls I see moving into the dorms have twice as many boxes."

She nodded, letting him think whatever he wanted. She didn't intend to explain this was all she owned in the entire world. She'd sold everything that was worth anything just to get Harold's horrendous debts paid.

"Thank you for your help. I'd offer you something to drink, but the fridge is empty."

"You're welcome. Guess we should have stocked that fridge for you." He chuckled. Heading for the door, he paused. "I'll see you tomorrow at nine for your training. Pete will be there also. He's the new RD for the freshmen men's dorm. You'll meet the three other women leaders as well."

Adelaide's heart dropped. Doubt assaulted her. "Yes, I'll see you then." Could she really do this job? Was she even capable?

At four o'clock the following morning, Adelaide crawled from her bed. She'd tossed and turned the entire night. She had three days of intense training ahead of her and prep for WOW—Week of Welcome, which would start bright and early Monday morning. "This is where the rubber meets the road, Adelaide," she spoke to her blurry-eyed image in the bathroom mirror. "I can do all things through Christ. . ." She repeated her biblical mantra of the past fourteen months.

Even dressing was a dilemma. Luckily, Chicago was two hours later, so at five she called Lissa for advice on what RAs and RDs normally wore and realized she owned nothing appropriate. Lissa promised to send a box. In the meantime, Adelaide would wear the most casual cotton skirt and blouse she owned with her one pair of flat sandals. Her confidence was shot by the time she left her little apartment at six a.m. for Starbucks. Her makeup was impeccable, as always, but she'd pulled her hair back into a ponytail at Lissa's instruction—a ponytail! And this outfit—if one could refer to it as such—was last worn when rummaging through the basement and discarding most of what she'd found. Truly she felt amazed it hadn't hit the Goodwill pile as well.

At Starbucks she ordered a mocha and headed for the comfy chair in the corner. There she pulled her Bible out of her bag to have some quiet time with God. Today she started a new book—Joshua. As she read chapter one, she realized that even though God had given the Israelites the promised land, they still had to fight for it. Was this job her promised land? Even so, she'd have to fight—the fear, the insecurity, and her own inadequacies. *I can do all things through Christ. . . .*

Adelaide arrived at the nine o'clock training almost half an hour early. She made her way to the conference room where her first interview had taken place. Of course no one was there yet. Being punctual had been important to Harold, and he'd ingrained the habit in her as well.

Noting the stacks of papers at the end of the table, she took a seat near the opposite end. Finally another woman— probably early thirties—breezed in. "Hello." She approached Adelaide, claiming the seat next to her. "I'm Rachel, the RD for the senior girls. You must be the new freshmen director."

Adelaide held out her hand. "Adelaide English. Pleased to meet you."

A young man came in and claimed the seat across from

the two women. He smiled at both of them but said nothing. Two girls, barely out of college, entered and also chose seats across the table. Isaiah sauntered in with Rose on his heels, followed seconds later by three more young men. *I'm so old. I can't do this.* Adelaide fought an overwhelming urge to run out the door and not stop until she hit the Texas state line.

Isaiah stood at the end of the table. "Today's training, as you can see, is for RDs. Tomorrow and Friday will incorporate RAs. I'd like to begin with a get-to-know-you exercise. Sort of like speed dating, our goal is to find out five facts about each person in this room. The first person to reach that goal has to jump up and down five times while yelling, 'I did it! I did it!' Then they have to read their fact list aloud so we can verify he or she actually won."

Great. Adelaide bit her bottom lip. She hated these sort of games. When Isaiah blew the whistle, she rose and went to the front of the room, grabbing a pad and pen like all the others were doing. Seemed everyone was grilling someone, except her.

"Addie." Isaiah motioned her over to him. "Start with me."

"I think I already know five facts about you."

He lifted his eyebrow. "Let's hear them."

"You are a professor. You teach the Bible. You hate sidewalks. You're a widower and have two sons."

"Impressive." He seemed surprised. "Now let's see if I can do you. You, Adelaide English, are a perfectionist, a widow, have a daughter, came from Dallas, and are fulfilling a childhood dream by attending the Lord's College."

She nodded and moved on. Instead of waiting her turn, she listened carefully as other people grilled each other and wrote the facts, moving on to another group. By eaves-dropping she actually gained the information faster than if she interviewed each person—sort of two for the price of one. When she finished, no one had done the "I did it" jump. She debated. Did she want to draw that sort of attention to herself? Her preference lay toward being unnoticed.

"You done?" So much for remaining unnoticed.

"Yes." She faced Isaiah. "Just getting ready to jump for joy." She forced herself to follow his instructions, trying to remember why she thought she'd make a good RD.

"Nicely done." Isaiah smiled.

His approval made the silly jumping and yelling worth it. Did he have any idea how starved she was for acceptance?

"Now if you will all take your seats, Addie will introduce each one of you with five facts we may or may not know."

She stood next to Isaiah at the head of the table. Her paper shook ever so slightly. Did anyone notice? She started with Dr. Shepherd and reiterated the facts she'd spoken aloud to him minutes ago. No one seemed surprised by anything she said. Then she introduced Shaun, Trei, Chase, and Pete—the boy's crew in order from seniors down to freshmen. She followed suit with the girl's crew.

"Rachel is in her thirties, unmarried, attended TLC a decade ago, stuck around to get her master's and then doctorate. Has held the same RD position for eleven years. Madalyn and Hayden both graduated last May, are the junior and sophomore RDs, have been best friends since junior high, are both in the master's program, and both want to be married by twenty-five at the latest."

"Thanks. Anyone disputing any of those facts?"

Several around the table shook their heads.

"Who wants to do the introductions of our winner?"

Nobody offered. Nobody could. Not one person had interviewed her. Talk about wanting to crawl under the closest rug. Adelaide's face burned, and she imagined it glowed red for all to see.

"Fine, I'll do it." He shot a compassionate glance her direction. "This is the newest member of our team—Adelaide English—or Addie, if you prefer. She hails from Dallas, Texas. . . ."

Adelaide watched each face as Isaiah rattled off her stats. Frankly, none of them cared. She was old enough to be most of their mothers. Who would want to know her better? Not one of them. They didn't even approach her. She'd never fit in here.

The rest of the day they went over the student handbook, read the rules, and talked about the responsibilities of a resident director. Her main job was to oversee the RAs and encourage them as Christians, as students, and as leaders. She'd also deal with any problems they couldn't handle and any bigger problems students might incur, like eating disorders, sexual misconduct, failing, and the like. *Why did I think I could do this?*

Adelaide slipped out the door the minute Dr. Shepherd said his last amen. She could bear no more torture.

The following morning, after a pep talk from Lissa and one from Monica, Adelaide ran into Dr. Shepherd as she walked past his office on her way to the conference room.

"Do you have a minute?" he asked as he exited through his door.

She nodded and stopped.

"Adelaide, I want you to work on becoming Addie."

His words of criticism were so familiar. "What do you mean exactly?"

He took her arm and pulled her out of the hallway and into his office. "You've got to relax. Look at you. You're as stiff as a board. I fear none of the students will feel comfortable with you until you're comfortable with yourself. None of the RDs appear to be bonding with you. The goal of the game yesterday was to get to know people. Did you have a single conversation with any of them?"

She shook her head, gaping at him. His reprimand stung. No man was ever happy with her. First her father picked and criticized, then Harold lectured and instructed, now she wasn't good enough for Isaiah Shepherd either. She stared at the floor and attempted to swallow the lump lodged in her throat. "I'm sorry."

"I don't want you to be sorry." He raised her chin with his index finger. "I'm only trying to help you." The words were tender. "I didn't mean to sound critical."

Nodding, she raised her eyes to meet his and knew he must see the tears glistening in their depths. Clearing her throat she said, "Thank you, Dr. Shepherd, for your guidance. I'm just embarrassed to have presented myself in such a light. I wanted to do a good job without having to be reprimanded."

He dropped his hand back to his side. "I'm not reprimanding you. It's just when you work with young adults, you need to be approachable."

"I'll try. I promise I'll change. Approachable. I can do that." She was babbling. "Is that all you wanted?"

He nodded, and she slipped out the door and into the bathroom. Locking herself in the nearest stall, she let a massive amount of tears fall. *Lord, I don't think I can do this. Please help me.* His criticism shot holes in her already sagging confidence and took her back to the little girl who never quite measured up.

After a good cry and then a long attempt to hide the repercussions with her makeup, Adelaide arrived just as day two of her torture began. Eight fifty-nine to be exact. Poor Harold must have just turned over in his grave. She was the last one to enter the very full room. One chair remained empty. The one on Dr. Shepherd's right. She slipped into it just as he stood to open the training with prayer. She sent up a prayer of her own. *Teach me to be approachable.* This job wasn't intended for an introvert. Why hadn't she considered that before?

Adelaide met the ten RAs who'd work with the freshmen girls in her dorm. There were Heather, Kim, Patti, Carol, Robin, Jessica, Sharon, Becky, Milla, and Erin. Heather rose to the top as a leader and helped Adelaide get the girls into the games. She was sort of the cheerleader of their group. As Isaiah had them compete in event after event that pitted them against other RDs and their teams, Heather encouraged them to try harder. She was one of the smaller girls but had a booming voice as she got into the competition. They didn't do a lot of talking on a personal level, but they did play hard and even won a couple of the games. Adelaide was exhausted and slept like a baby that night.

The third and final day of training was actually preparing for WOW. They had signs to paint, agendas to plan, and names and faces to memorize. They all worked together, yet each RA sort of did her own thing for her own hall. Adelaide was there to assist in any way possible. Most of them had thought out what they would do and didn't need much guidance. Robin was her shyest girl, and they clicked immediately. Two introverts in a sea of extroverts. Robin was doing this for her parents' sake to save them some money, so she—like Adelaide—had to push herself way beyond her comfort zone. Mostly, Adelaide made herself available and ended up playing gofer—running from one girl to the next, grabbing tape, getting more paint, or filling whatever need they had.

And then there was Isaiah—lurking, watching. And every time she looked into those nut-brown eyes of his, she sensed his disappointment. Was there a man alive who accepted a woman just how she was without trying to remake her?

The Monday following Week of Welcome, Adelaide went to her first class, Old Testament Survey with Dr. Shepherd. So far he'd turned out to be nothing like her first impression. She'd spent much of the past two weeks contemplating why she wanted this man to like and respect her. Other than the obvious fact that no man had ever done either where she was concerned, she realized she really liked and respected Isaiah.

She settled into a seat near the middle of the classroom. Something about him intrigued her, and she knew just what it was. The way he spoke of his deceased wife had tugged at her heartstrings. She'd spent her whole marriage longing for Harold to cherish her, and it was obvious that Dr. Shepherd had cherished his wife.

Adelaide glanced around the classroom. As always since arriving in Idaho, she was the oldest one here. Forty-five felt more ancient all the time. How could she ever keep up with these kids in their late teens or early twenties? Her memory didn't work as well as it once had. Once upon a time, she'd been the queen of trivial knowledge. Now? Not so much. She could barely remember what she had for lunch yesterday.

Glancing at her hands folded on the desk in front of her, they barely looked familiar, but they reminded her of her mother. Lissa's hands now looked like Adelaide's should. Time had a funny way of changing things and people. She was barely keeping up with a job she'd not been cut out for, and now she'd have to keep up with classes and homework, too? Why didn't Monica tell her she'd lost her mind instead of supporting this stupid, stupid decision?

"Welcome to Old Testament Survey," Isaiah interrupted her latest "freak-out," as Lissa called them. "Together we will study the Old Testament and observe how God has always pointed us to Jesus since time began." He took his place at the podium.

After introductions and a few opening comments, his first lecture of the new school year flowed forth, and the rest of the world ceased to exist for Adelaide. Isaiah's passion for sharing truth from God's Word entranced her. The hour flew. She wrote as fast as her pen would move.

She wanted to tell him what a wonderful speaker he was, but she was afraid of sounding like some sort of groupie, so she opted to slip out quietly.

"Adelaide?"

So much for an inconspicuous exit. "Yes?"

"May I walk you to chapel? Show you the best seats in the house?"

"Sure." What else could she say? "You're a wonderful teacher," she blurted, feeling her face flame. Thankful they were walking, she hoped he wouldn't notice her embarrassment.

"And you are my most conscientious student, writing down almost every word of my lecture as fast as possible. I'm impressed."

"My only hope of remembering." She smiled up at him. "I stick out like a sore thumb, don't I?" Adelaide felt so lost and hadn't realized how hard it would be to fit into college life at her age. The kids looked at her like she had three eyes.

He chuckled. "You're much prettier than a sore thumb."

Her face grew warm again. *Do you really think I'm pretty, or are you just being polite?* His opinion mattered more than she cared to admit.

Isaiah took her elbow and directed her to two empty seats along the aisle. She tried to relax and take in her surroundings. The chapel seated fifteen hundred, so it was by no means small. As she studied each stained-glass window, the beauty and serenity touched her. The piano and flute playing quietly in the background calmed her.

The service started with student-led contemporary praise and worship. Then the college president took the podium. Adelaide's thoughts wandered to the man seated beside her. He wore his standard fare: a pair of fairly new blue jeans, a baby blue oxford shirt with the first couple of buttons undone and chest hair peeking out, and a pair of Nike running shoes. Rugged and manly, Dr. Isaiah Shepherd was not at all the polished, manicured man Harold had been. Being with Isaiah made her feel like she'd missed something wonderful in her life.

Those thoughts not only frightened her, they mortified her.

four

"The one constant across the U.S. in general and in my life in particular is Starbucks. I'm on my way to meet Linda there now, but think about it, in a world miles and lifestyles apart, Dallas versus Coeur d'Alene, I can still sit in my favorite spot, surrounded by familiar scents and colors and furniture, and have my same favorite drink. It tastes the same, smells the same, and that makes me feel secure somehow."

"Starbucks always was your weakness." Lissa giggled. "Guess where I am right at this moment?"

"Starbucks?"

"You got it."

"I trained you well."

"You've been spending a lot of time with Linda. I'm glad God's given you a friend."

"Me, too. She invites me to coffee a couple of times a week. I sit with her and Walt in church. It's nice. Hey, I'm here."

"That was quick."

"It's only about a mile or two from the college, but it's in this new upscale area. They have waterfront condos that I'd love to live in."

"I'm sure they beat the dorm." Lissa giggled again, and Adelaide squeezed her eyes shut, relishing her daughter's laughter.

"I love you, Lis. Talk to you tomorrow."

"I love you, Mom, and I'm so proud."

Adelaide closed her phone and laid it against her heart.

41

She swallowed hard and checked her appearance in the rearview mirror. She quickly reapplied her lipstick.

Linda waited in one of their two favorite chairs—the oversized ones tucked in the corner. Two hot drinks rested on the table between them. Adelaide settled into the other chair, catching a whiff of her vanilla latte.

"Good morning." Linda closed the Bible sitting on her lap.

"Morning." Adelaide picked up her cup, holding it near her nose and breathing in one of her favorite scents in all the world. Then she took a long, slow sip and let the warm liquid roll down her throat.

"So how's it going? Do you feel like you're settling into a routine?"

Adelaide's mind ran over the past couple of weeks. "More unsettled and uncertain than routine, but hopefully soon."

"It will come. I just so admire what you're doing. You're very courageous."

Adelaide smiled and smoothed her hand over her denim skirt. *If you only knew the truth—my insides are a pile of Jell-O most of the time.*

"Cute skirt, by the way."

"My daughter mailed it to me, but I can't believe I'm wearing denim. I had a fight with myself this morning. Nylons or no nylons? 'No' won out, so I'm nylon-less. Can you believe it?"

Laughing and shaking her head, Linda said, "I haven't worn nylons for the better part of a decade. They are history in this part of the country."

"You probably think I'm crazy stressing over pantyhose."

"Not at all. We women stress over our appearance all the time. Take me just this morning—do I wear my beige sandals, which are more comfortable, or do I dress the slacks up a bit with a heel? In other words, do I choose comfort or style?"

Linda lifted her pant leg, and the beige sandals had won out. "For me, comfort outweighs style ninety percent of the time."

A pang of envy shot through Adelaide. She'd never even considered comfort. Appearance was everything to Harold.

"Speaking of comfort, jeans are the appropriate dress for Zay's administrative staff get-together."

"Oh, I'm not planning on going." She'd weighed the invitation from every angle and decided to stay home.

"What?" Linda raised a brow. "Why not?"

"I won't know anyone well and am not much of a conversationalist."

"Hey, I resent that. You know me and Walt," she chided.

"You know what I mean."

Then Lissa's voice whispered in Adelaide's memory. *As you're reinventing yourself, Mom, be real. You don't have to be that plastic person anymore.*

Adelaide raised her chin and sucked in a deep breath. "I've spent years attending social events to meet just the right people. They are filled with meaningless conversations trying to impress. I'm done with all that."

Linda assessed her for several seconds. "Fair enough, but this is nothing like you're describing. This is a group of coworkers coming together for a day of fun. It's as unpretentious as a day can get. Horseshoes, croquet, badminton, and fried chicken. Blue jeans and tennis shoes all the way, girlfriend. None of that uppity stuff. Just Christian fellowship. It's a great time for you to get to know more people—nice people."

As she listened to Linda's reasoning, Adelaide decided to attend. After all, part of reinventing yourself was making new friends. "Jeans and tennis shoes?"

Linda nodded and laughed. "You make them sound distasteful. Do you even own a pair?"

"In that box my daughter sent is some—as she calls them—'more appropriate' college attire. She made me promise to bury my pearls in the bottom of my jewelry box until Christmas vacation."

"Sounds like good advice." Linda glanced at her wristwatch. "I've got to run. My boss values punctuality. How about if Walt and I pick you up tomorrow about noon?"

Adelaide rose. "I'll be the one in denim pants and a pair of Nikes—in case you fail to recognize me."

Linda wore an amused expression, gave Adelaide a quick hug, and raced out the door.

This would give her a natural way to get to know the other RDs better. She needed some advice on how to get her girls to warm up to her. They were polite, distant, and seemingly uninterested in much relationship. She'd hoped to click with them as she had with Lissa's friends, but it hadn't happened yet. They'd had two Monday night meetings at her place, and as soon as business was over, they were out of there. Except Robin—sweet, quiet, unassuming Robin.

ಜ

Isaiah glanced up from the grill, where he'd lined up about fifty ears of corn. *Was that. . .?* He did a double take. Sure enough, Addie was climbing out of the backseat of Walt and Linda's sedan. Wow. She looked good in jeans. His heart did a funny little beat. He'd not been attracted to a woman in a decade, and here this little Texas filly drew him in like no one but Julie ever had. Man, would he love to see her set free.

"Off-limits there, buddy." James glanced from him to Adelaide and back again. "You know the policy on staff dating staff. A big no-no."

"Her? Are you kidding? She is so not my type." All true, but the chemistry still bubbled. He glanced at the three of them walking toward him. "Not my type at all." He returned his attention to the corn, and James made a beeline toward the president and his wife as they exited their sedan.

When they reached the grill, he and Walt shook hands, he kissed Linda's cheek, and then there was Addie. What to do? She held out her hand, which he accepted. Soft. Warm. Small. And electrifying.

"Glad you came."

"You sound surprised."

"Didn't mean to, but I wasn't sure you'd make it."

"I almost didn't." Glancing at Linda, she smiled.

"It took a bit of persuading, but she's here. And I know we're all pleased to have her on staff, so she should be here." Linda's eyes met his and challenged him to speak up.

"She's right, and I, for one, am glad you're here. It's a day of fun and bonding and important for all staff to attend. Welcome to your first annual TLC picnic."

"Zay, the corn." Walt pointed to the smoking grill.

"That's rich coming from you. Excuse me." He quickly turned each ear. Some had a few black kernels, but most survived the near miss.

"What can I help with?" Linda asked.

"Rose is in the kitchen. You can check with her." He continued flipping ears at a fast pace.

"She always helps him with the picnic," Linda told Addie. "Shall we join her and see if she can use four extra hands?"

Addie nodded, and the women headed toward the house.

"How do you think she's working out?" Walt asked with concern in his voice.

"I'm trying to get her to loosen up, but honestly, the RAs aren't warming up to her like I'd hoped. I'm attempting to soften her, but she's so stiff and formal."

"Linda's working on her, too. She really likes her and has great hope."

Ear by ear, Zay removed the corn with his tongs. "I just wanted to give her a break. I hope I don't regret my decision."

Walt sighed. "I hope not, too, bud."

***

Adelaide followed Linda toward the rambling ranch house set on a grassy knoll. A pine-covered mountain stood tall and proud behind Zay's house.

"Don't you love his giant Christmas tree?" Linda gestured toward a pine tree standing perfectly in front of his house near the center.

Adelaide paused, touching the spiny needles. "They always smell so wonderful." She sucked in a deep breath of pine. "Fresh and alive. Did someone plant it here?"

"I think his wife planted it there before she died. They still decorate it every year."

How different they were. Isaiah wanted to remember, and she wanted to forget.

Linda pointed to an A-frame off to the left. "He built that for his mother-in-law. She came and stayed while Julie battled cancer."

"This is a nice place. How much land does he have?"

"I think about twenty acres. Past the A-frame and about halfway down the hill to the left, he has a barn and his prize horses."

"I love horses." She'd grown up with horses at her grand-parents' farm and some days still longed for the joy they'd brought her as a child.

"I'm sure Zay will take you on a tour later. His horses are his pride and joy, and he loves showing them off."

Once in the kitchen, Adelaide admired the large modern

area—a dream for any woman who loved to cook.

"This kitchen has every convenience known to man. Both Julie and Zay loved to entertain."

"So did Harold, only we had everything catered."

Rose had finished frying the chicken, so they helped her carry it and the potato salad out to the area where the tables were set up. The red-checked table covers reminded Adelaide again of her grandparents.

"Where is everyone? This is a lot of food for the ten or so people I've seen so far."

"Come on, I'll show you." Linda led her around the house to where about thirty more people were playing various games, laughing, yelling, and jiving each other.

"So this picnic isn't for everyone that works at the college?"

"No, just the admin team. Can you imagine if all the professors came? Oh my goodness. I don't think Zay's place would be big enough."

"Seems like a lot of staff for twelve hundred or so students."

"You'd be surprised how many people it requires to run a small Christian college." Then she turned to face the group of game players. "Everybody. . . ," Linda said, raising her voice. "Chow's on." She glanced at Adelaide. "You can spot the competitive ones. They'd rather finish their game than eat."

Adelaide followed Linda through the serving line. She sat at a picnic table surrounded by Walt, Linda, Isaiah—was she comfortable calling him Zay yet?—and Rose. She ate in silence, listening to the idle chitchat surrounding her. She needed to approach at least Rachel but hadn't worked up her nerve. Since Rachel was the next oldest RD, maybe she could direct Adelaide. "The food was wonderful." She laid down her fork.

"Yes, it was," Walt agreed, patting his stomach.

"Thanks to our wonderful chefs—Zay and Rose." Linda

pushed her plate away.

Adelaide turned her gaze to Isaiah. "How many years have you been doing this picnic?"

"We started the year after Julie died. Some people"—Isaiah glanced pointedly at Linda—"thought I needed a diversion from all my grief."

Linda nodded. "We all did. So it's been about nine years." She drew her brows together for a moment and then nodded. "Yep, I think this is actually the tenth admin staff picnic."

"A lot of picnics." Rose started clearing plates. One man who looked familiar, but Adelaide didn't know his name, challenged the crowd to a game of horseshoes. Adelaide noticed Linda whisper something to Isaiah.

He nodded and turned to Adelaide. "Would you like a tour of the barn?"

She fought off the prideful response of saying no. She didn't like the way Linda pushed them together. "Sure."

Isaiah rose, and she followed. He led her past the guest house, where she caught her first glimpse of his stable area. Wow. She'd not expected such a beautiful, state-of-the-art facility.

He unlocked the door and waited for her to step through. Horses, hay, and leather scents mixed together and carried her back to summers at her grandparents'. The joy of childhood memories settled over her. She closed her eyes to savor it all a moment longer.

"You okay?"

"Just enjoying the smell of the barn. It's been a long time."

"You're full of surprises." He led her down the center hall toward the paddocks. "So underneath it all, you're a farm girl at heart?" He raised his brow, and Adelaide was certain it was disbelief.

"What? I don't remind you of a barn-loving girl?"

He studied her. "Nope. I missed that one completely." He stopped in front of a beautiful sorrel with a white blaze down the center of her face. "This is my best mare."

"She's gorgeous." Adelaide scratched behind the mare's ears. She tipped her head toward Adelaide's hand.

Isaiah shook his head. A bit of wonder settled into his expression. "This girl delivers top-notch foals."

Adelaide ran her palm down the blaze. "Do you run some sort of horse farm?" She glanced up at the man standing next to her, admiring his strong jaw.

"Thoroughbreds. Top bloodlines, cream-of-the-crop thoroughbreds. One of my colts won the Derby last year."

Adelaide's breath whooshed from her. "The Derby?" Her hand dropped as if the horse suddenly had a contagious disease.

"As in Kentucky. Surely you've heard of it. Most city folks have," he taunted in a light tone.

Oh she'd heard all right. So had her big-money, high-betting husband.

৵

He'd said something wrong. Addie's whole demeanor changed. Her gaze accused him of something—something akin to treason—but he wasn't sure what.

"You own a thoroughbred breeding farm?" It sounded more like an accusation than a question.

Zay nodded. "Yep. I've been dabbling in horse breeding for a couple of decades and have refined my line to such a point that they're in high demand."

"I see. I think I'm ready to go back to the fun and games." Her expression was pleasant, but the throbbing pulse in her clenched jaw led him to believe he'd somehow offended her.

"Sure." He gave the mare one last pat. "I thought you liked horses."

"I do. I love horses."

"Would you want to ride with me sometime?"

"No thank you." Miss Prim, Proper, Pillow Fluffer had returned. The walk back to the crowd would have chilled an Eskimo.

About halfway to their destination, he stopped. "Wait."

She did as he asked and turned to face him. Her expression was pleasant and unreadable, but her tight lips indicated something more.

"Did I do something to offend you?"

She shook her head. "How could you offend me? We barely know each other."

He shrugged, shoving his hands deep into the pockets of his jeans. "I have no idea."

"Could you point me in the direction of the ladies' room?"

Isaiah gave her directions and watched her walk up the hill toward his home. *Women!*

"Did you invite her to go riding with you sometime?" Linda asked as he strode up to her and Walt.

"I did."

"And. . ." Linda cocked her head to the side.

"You've been single too long if you've forgotten women want details—not one-word answers." Walt snickered.

"I guess I have." Isaiah turned to Linda. "I asked. She turned me down." He shrugged.

"Turned you down? She loves horses. You have some. What's to turn down?"

He spotted Adelaide disappearing into his house. No matter how much he'd hoped to change her into an Addie, inside still lurked Adelaide. Always cool, always distant, always composed Adelaide.

&

"But, Mom, I thought you said he was cute." Frustration laced each of Lissa's words.

"What does that have to do with anything? He raises racehorses! How can a Christian raise racehorses? Doesn't he know that horse racing leads to gambling and gambling destroys lives?" A wave of grief hit Adelaide and almost dynamited her composure.

"So that's what this is about," Lissa spoke softly. "Just because he raises horses doesn't mean he gambles. And you need to forgive Dad. He messed up bad, but he never meant to destroy our lives."

Forgive? How?

"Of course you're right, Lis. I'm sorry I lost sight of that for a moment. Hey, hon, homework calls. Can we finish this conversation later?"

After closing her cell phone, she screamed into the square aqua pillow adorning her sofa. "I hate you, Harold. Do you hear me? I hate you!" A tsunami of self-pity pulled at her, threatening to drag her into an abyss she'd never find her way out of.

five

Adelaide gazed out her window. It was a beautiful campus. Tall stately trees towered above the dignified brick buildings. Green grass carpeted the grounds. There was a true sense of peace within the college.

And she found peace here as well—except for Isaiah. Although she was drawn to him in many ways, including his godly teaching, his rugged appeal, and his kindness, she found herself repelled by his hobby. Working on being real, she had no idea how she should even act around him, so most of the time she avoided him altogether. But some days, like today, she just longed to be near him. The confusion was driving her crazy. One thing for sure, he was her best teacher. He created in his students a hunger to know the Bible better and to know God more.

Her ringing cell drew her out of her introspection. Her caller ID indicated it was Kim, one of her RAs.

"Mrs. English—"

"Please, just Adelaide. Or Heather calls me Mrs. E." *Will they ever see me like Isaiah wants them to?*

"Sorry—Adelaide, I need you to sub for me on Roommate Date Saturday. I've got a fever and sore throat. Don't worry—it'll be fun."

"Sub for you?" Adelaide hoped Kim didn't notice the panic in her voice.

"You just chaperone. No big deal."

No big deal? She'd never done anything like that before.

"I'll have Heather come by with the 411. Thanks. You're a lifesaver."

Adelaide closed her cell. Since arriving here at the college, she'd been stretched for sure. "I can do this. I can—all things through Christ. . ." She said the words with force, hating that everything new scared her to death because she might fail, might not do it right or well.

She'd seen the flyers and heard the girls discussing the roommate date event, but honestly hadn't paid a whole lot of attention. After all, until three minutes ago it didn't affect her much. And just keeping up with homework, classes, and meetings was keeping her up to all hours of the night. Those all-night study sessions were much harder than they'd been a couple of decades earlier.

A knock on her door drew Adelaide to her feet. When she opened it, in marched Heather. "Hi, Mrs. E.," the petite blond greeted her.

Adelaide hid her doubts. "Chaperone. So explain what I do, where I go, the time, etcetera."

"Will do." Heather handed her a gold flyer. "Each RA is responsible for the girls in her wing. It's a really fun day—so fun. You'll love it!"

Adelaide wasn't feeling the love at the moment.

"Every girl who participates is set up on a date by her roommate. We take the bus to Memorial Field for a day of fun and games. All sorts of competitions."

Adelaide nodded. More competitions. "So what do I do?"

"Show up." Heather laughed. "Seriously, not much. Because it's a school-sanctioned event, chaperones are required. Sort of old-fashioned, I know, but that's TLC—conservative to the core."

Heather talked fast and stopped to catch her breath before

filling Adelaide in on the time and place to catch the bus. "Bring a book and sunscreen and you'll be good," the girl promised. "Unless. . ." Her eyes sparkled. "We set *you* up on a date. Then you get to participate."

Get to? "I'll be happy as can be sitting on the sidelines. I can do that. No date necessary. I promise. Got it?" For once, confidence oozed out in her words.

"Yep, I've got it. No date. I'll see you Saturday in front of the gym at ten in the morning."

"I'll be there, book in tow." This might even be fun and definitely a chance to get to know her girls better. Adelaide closed the door behind Heather—glad Heather understood the no-date request.

&

"You want me to what?" Isaiah glanced up from the stack of paperwork on his desk to focus on Heather Norris, one of Addie's RAs.

"I want you to escort Mrs. E. on the roommate date. You are still single, right?"

He sighed, hoping he'd somehow misunderstood. "That I am, but I'm not sure this is such a grand idea. Why don't you let me off the hook this time?"

"No way. You know the rules. She's single, you're single—"

"But you're not her roommate."

Heather smiled, showing the dimple in her cheek. "Nope, but since she doesn't have one, I put myself in charge of seeing that she doesn't go alone."

Well, maybe this is my chance to see how she interacts with her RAs. And my chance to encourage her.

"Come on," Heather persisted. "It's only one day. Besides, it humanizes you to interact with students."

"Humanizes? Do they think I'm an alien?"

"Well, sometimes. You get all passionate about the Lord and you seem lofty and way above the rest of us. This gives us all a chance to see you're just a regular guy."

"All right. Count me in. I hope you plan to tell Adelaide this was a complete setup and totally your idea."

She winked. "I'll take care of everything. See you Saturday." And she was gone. He wondered how she'd gotten past Rose and waltzed in unannounced.

A short while later, he met Walt and Linda for lunch. "Guess what I got roped into on Saturday?" He filled them in on Heather's visit.

"Does Adelaide know?" Linda's brows drew together.

"I have no idea, but I'm not telling her. She'll find out on Saturday, and I'm sure she'll be beyond thrilled." He paused. "Why do you look so worried?"

"Oh, no reason." She was suddenly nonchalant about the whole idea.

The waiter appeared, and the conversation dropped. Isaiah thought back to Adelaide's sudden change in attitude when they were at his house. He guessed Walt and Linda knew something, but they weren't talking. He figured he'd find out soon enough.

❧

Adelaide stood in the parking lot with what seemed like half of the college population. It would be easy to lose herself in this crowd. Each wing had an assigned meeting spot, and she found hers.

Heather joined her in line to board the bus. "I have a surprise for you."

Adelaide turned to face the girl. And there he stood— Isaiah. If only the pavement could swallow her alive. Without Heather saying it, Adelaide knew she had a date—the one and only man she'd love to avoid.

"Good morning, Addie."

"Morning, Dr. Shepherd."

"Zay."

"This was totally my idea," Heather assured her. "He so wants you to know he had nothing to do with this little arrangement."

Adelaide glanced at Isaiah. Heather's blunt honesty caused him to look uncomfortable.

"So he doesn't want to go either?" She gazed from Heather to him.

"Sure, I'll go."

Adelaide noticed he didn't say he wanted to go—he just said he would.

"Sounds delightful," Adelaide lied. She pasted her plastic smile on her face—the one she'd perfected over the years. Truthfully, nothing about spending a day with this man appealed—maybe if he had a different hobby, but she had learned to fake her way through many a social event.

They climbed the steps onto one of the big yellow buses they'd rented from the local school district. Adelaide slipped into the first available seat, and Isaiah slid in next to her. His long legs barely fit in the space available. He was a large man, and the confined space accentuated his tall, muscular build. They sat shoulder to shoulder, and Adelaide tried to relax. She searched for a neutral conversation starter.

"Do you like competition?" Maybe he'd sit on the sidelines with her.

He grinned down at her, and her insides jolted.

"Love it, so you can plan on winning today."

"I'm not very good at new things. I think I'll just watch."

"You do realize all the events are designed for couples?"

Couples? "You're kidding. Heather told me to bring a good book." She pulled it from her tote to verify her plans. "I really don't do games." The panicked feeling she was so accustomed to rose up, turning her insides into a quivering mass.

"I'll help you. It'll be fine."

Mom, reinvent you. Don't give in to your old patterns and habits. Be who you want to be. Be who you are. You have so much to offer.

Dare she? Did she have anything to offer? She glanced at her partner for the day. In spite of his association with gambling, he was a nice man. An attractive man. The word *hunk* provided an apt description.

Once they unloaded from the bus, they all lined up by wing. The student body president was the emcee. His voice echoed over Memorial Field. "Let the games begin! The first competition is the three-legged race, and remember, there are awesome prizes for the winning couple of each event and the couple with the most points overall at the end of the day."

"I plan on making at least one of those prizes mine." Adelaide noted the competitive edge in Isaiah's voice.

"Maybe you should find a new partner. I don't want to hold you back from your lofty goals." Her words sounded light, but she didn't want him to be mad at her—she'd seen enough of Harold's wrath to last her two lifetimes.

"No way. You're stuck with me for the rest of the day." He grinned, and his appeal only increased.

"I'm not good at competition."

"If you can't do it perfectly, why bother?"

"Exactly." *But how did you know?* She worked hard at not being transparent. *In Christ, it should be the opposite.*

"Don't worry." He used the long strip of cotton they'd been given and tied his right leg to her left. "I won't shoot you or anything if we lose. Now let's practice." He pulled her against his side and wrapped his arm around her waist. "When I say go, we'll start with our loose legs. It's easy once you get the hang of it."

They sort of stumbled a couple of steps. "So you say."

He laughed at their feeble attempt, and she giggled. What a relief that he wasn't angry.

They hobbled in a little circle. The field was crowded, so there wasn't much room for practice.

At the whistle, everyone moved to the starting line. "I do like to win, but if we don't, it's cool. I don't want you to feel bad."

His reassurance touched her. Today she wanted to be a fun, enjoyable, and attractive woman. Glancing down at her blue-jean-clad legs, she smiled at how far she'd come. Yes, today she'd go beyond fun—she'd be the girl she'd dreamed of being but had never dared. Poor Harold would probably turn over in his grave. That alone might make it worth it.

"On your mark, get set." The whistle blew. Isaiah pretty much carried her. Her right foot barely skimmed the ground. Something about the picture reminded her of God and the way He'd carried her through the time since Harold's death. He'd held her close just as Isaiah did now.

They didn't win, but finished in the top three. They each received a five-dollar gift card to Starbucks.

"We'll go together sometime. Winning feels good, doesn't it?"

She rolled her eyes.

❧

Holding her close against him felt right. It had been a long time, such a long time. He'd nearly forgotten.

He stretched his neck from side to side. *Refocus.* "What event is next?" he asked the couple standing next to them.

"Potato sack race, only this is done as a team event."

"How?"

"Each person has their own sack, but then you have to be connected on one side by not only holding your own bag, but also your partner's."

Isaiah nodded. "We can do that, right?"

"Absolutely." She was more relaxed than he'd ever seen her. Today was good for her.

The burlap sacks were being passed out, and he grabbed two. Addie took hers and stepped in, pulling it up to about her waist. Because of his height, his only came up to his hips. He lined himself up right next to her, and they each grabbed hold of the other's gunnysack.

Together they hopped to the starting line.

"I think I'm too old for this." Addie laughed a breathless sound.

Again the emcee shouted, "On your mark, get set. . ." and blew the whistle.

Isaiah made a huge hop to get their momentum going. Only problem, Addie's hop wasn't nearly as long. The force of his lunge with his hold on her sack caused her to lose her balance. She tumbled over like a house made of dominoes. He tried to catch her, but that only exacerbated the problem, and he ended up getting his feet tangled in the burlap bag and fell, too.

Addie lay in a heap, laughing, and he lay next to her doing the same. Something about that moment clinched it for him. He was crazy about her—the sound of her laughter, the smell of her perfume, the feel of her skin.

The race was over long before either of them made any effort to get up. He took his time sitting up. He'd not soon forget the vision of her lying in the grass, a huge smile on her face and the shadow of pain missing from her eyes. No, he'd treasure this moment for a long while.

He held his hand out to her. She took it, and he pulled her into a sitting position.

"You're not going to win any prizes down here, big fellow." Her eyes sparkled in merriment.

Unbeknownst to her, he'd already won the biggest prize of all—a day with her. A day he'd dreaded was now a day he'd cherish for quite some time.

He picked some grass from her hair. Her breathing changed, and she sat very still. Her gaze connected with his. Her lips parted, so slightly, so subtly.

We can't kiss. Not ever, but certainly not here. He jumped up, nearly getting his feet tangled in the sack a second time.

"We've got to get ready for the next event." He pulled her to her feet.

"I better not end up on the ground again," she threatened in a gruff voice. Did she feel any of the disappointment he did? Guess he'd never know.

They walked over to the emcee area to check on the next event. "The water balloon toss," Isaiah read off the poster. He turned to her. "Don't let me down."

"Right back at you there."

"You're a tough talker. You ever done this before?"

She shook her head. "You?"

"I have, so listen up."

She saluted him. Where had this playful, fun-loving woman been hiding?

"Seriously, I'm a pro at this. The trick is to throw and catch it lightly. Think you can handle it?"

"How does one catch lightly when one doesn't actually catch at all?"

"You can't catch?"

"Rarely."

"Just hold your arms like this out in front of you." He gave her a demonstration. "I'll toss it right into your hands."

"I'm just giving Mr. Competitive a hard time. I'm a tennis player and actually can hold my own with a ball. Should I be worried about you, though?"

"Yeah, right."

She giggled.

They walked over to where the next competition was scheduled to start. She lined up across from him, about two feet away. As the balloons were passed out, Addie was handed a purple one. When the whistle blew, she tossed it to him.

"Nice gentle toss. Good job." Only one team busted their balloon. His side of the line was directed to take a step back. This time he tossed it to Addie. She caught it like a pro.

This continued until there were only four teams left, and they were now five or six feet apart. He had the balloon. It was tough to toss it that far and be gentle at the same time. The whistle blew. One guy overthrew and soaked his gal. Another didn't give it enough oomph, and it splattered at his partner's feet.

Addie caught theirs with precision. They now had a prize in the bag. He could taste first place.

She stepped back and threw. He had to stretch forward to catch the swooshing orb. It almost didn't make it, but did. Unfortunately, so did the other team's.

He put too much power behind his next throw. He knew it the second he released the balloon. It sailed at Addie, too fast for her to catch it. She tried, though. It burst on impact, soaking the front of her.

Her mouth opened wide. "You did that on purpose." She grabbed the last surviving balloon from the champion and threw it hard and fast in his direction.

He turned to run but wasn't quick enough. She caught him with the water-filled balloon square in the back.

His impulse was to chase her until he caught her and kiss that smug expression right off her face. Again, not an option, so he joined the crowd in laughter. Today would go far in connecting uptight Addie to the students. They were awarded a gift certificate to a local eatery for their second-place finish.

"Now we have to get together twice," he informed her, careful not to say the "date" word.

"That, my friend, is a real bummer."

The emcee announced the pizza had finally arrived. He and Addie made their way through the line. She greeted Jessica, one of her RAs. There wasn't a lot of connection—both seemed uncertain what to say. After grabbing their pizza and soda, he led her away from the crowd and up into the bleachers where they could get to know each other better.

six

They settled a few rows up the bleachers. He juggled their pizza, and she carried two cans of soda. He slid into the row a ways and straddled the metal seat. She sat down facing forward, setting the sodas between them. He handed her a plate with two decent-size slices of pepperoni pizza on it.

"Thank you." She brushed a strand of hair off her cheek.

"Tell me about you. Did you always live in Texas?" He popped the top on his Coke.

"No, my father was military, so I lived many places growing up. What about you? You mentioned Wisconsin and LA. Is that it besides here?"

"Yep. My parents still live in the same house I grew up in. I try to get back a couple of times a year to help Dad with projects. He shouldn't be climbing on the roof or things like that at his age." He sipped his soda. "Where are your parents now?"

"They've both passed on."

"I'm sorry." Compassion filled his voice and eyes.

"Thanks." *Sadly, we were never close anyway.* But she didn't want to talk about herself. "Any siblings to help you with those roof-type projects?"

"One sister. She lives just a few miles from Mom and Dad. She takes care of their day-to-day needs, and I cover the bigger stuff."

"Sounds like a good system." She and Isaiah were as different as summer and winter, yet she found herself really enjoying their time together.

He'd finished his pizza and laid his wadded napkin on his empty paper plate. "Do you have siblings?"

"Two brothers. They both followed my dad's lead and are career military." *Haven't seen either of them in years.*

She gazed out over the crowd of couples filling the field below.

"What do you think of Coeur d'Alene?"

She took her time answering. "I love the college and am enjoying my classes very much. The homework is sometimes overwhelming. I don't think my brain functions as well as it once did. The campus is gorgeous, so green. As for the town, what the place lacks in amenities, it makes up for in charm. The shops downtown are adorable and unique. I do miss having a megamall, but am so thankful for the Starbucks that I can let it slide."

He laughed. "Do I detect an addiction?"

"You do, and I won't deny it. One a day keeps me happy and running in top condition." She laid her napkin across the now-empty paper plate. "How did you and your wife end up here?"

"I got a job at the college. Started in the maintenance area and worked my way through my master's and doctorate programs. We came sight unseen, not knowing what to expect. We were both a little uncertain, expecting fields of potatoes everywhere."

Adelaide laughed. "Me, too, and I've yet to see one potato, except on my plate."

"Most of the potato farming is in the southeastern part of the state. And this is one of the most beautiful areas of Idaho. Julie and I both fell in love with the place immediately. That's why I took an upper-level job at the college when I finished my grad work. We were both avid hikers, skiers, hunters, and fishermen. This place had it all—still does." He glanced up into the clear blue sky.

A pang of regret shot through Adelaide—not because of what he and his wife shared but because of what she and Harold hadn't. She'd tried so hard to find some common ground to build their lives around, but never succeeded. And honestly, he never seemed interested. As long as she and the house looked good, he was content.

"Can I ask you something?" Isaiah broke the silence.

As long as it's not personal. She shrugged.

"What happened a couple of weeks ago when you were at my house? One minute you were loving the horses, and the next you were—I don't know—angry, annoyed, something." His brows drew together, and he shook his head.

All the feelings from that afternoon returned. How could she make him understand without saying too much? Without revealing too much of her personal life and her husband's gambling addiction? She traced the seam of her jeans with her eyes. Finally she raised her head and took a deep breath, torn between honesty and a "Harold response." *Be real. Be real. Be real.* Lissa's words kept pounding in her head.

"I don't like gambling. With it comes heartache and destruction. Many innocent people pay a high price for someone else's stupidity."

"I agree and don't like gambling myself. Nor do I gamble." He studied her intently.

She wondered what he saw—all the pain, hurt, vulnerability. She hoped not. "But you breed racehorses." Her words rang of accusation.

"Oh, I get it. You think I contribute to the problem." He sat up straighter.

"Well, you do, don't you?" Her voice had risen in both

volume and pitch since the beginning of their conversation.

"So if I grew grapes, I'd be contributing to alcoholism?"

"In a roundabout way."

"This is ridiculous." He shook his head. "I raise horses. I sell them, but not every horse ends up on a track. What the buyer does with them is their choice, not mine." He studied her face again. "But you're not convinced."

She shook her head. "Sorry, but no."

"So in your eyes, I'm responsible for every gambler out there?"

Put like that, it sounded silly. "Not exactly, but whatever causes your brother to stumble, you should avoid."

He stretched his neck from side to side. "I raise horses. I do not run a racetrack or a gambling casino, nor am I a bookie."

"I know this sounds foolish to you, but it's a hill to die on for me."

He sighed. "Adelaide, what if you sold your car, and the new owner drove drunk and killed someone. Would you be responsible?"

"That's different." Why couldn't he get it? "I didn't intentionally sell my car to be used in that way."

"And I don't intentionally sell horses so they cause people to gamble. If I quit selling horses, would the world's gambling problem be solved?"

"Five minutes until this afternoon's competition begins," blasted over the loudspeakers.

"I'm sorry that you don't understand my point of view, nor do I understand yours."

He rose, picking up their trash from the bench. "I guess we'll have to agree to disagree. Friends don't always see eye to eye on everything, right?"

She nodded her acceptance of his statement, but the

comment hit her dead-on. Was she so close-minded that she couldn't be friends with someone who had an opinion other than her own? Honestly, she didn't know. Other than Monica back in Texas, she had no true friends—people who knew the ugly truths of her life and loved her anyway. At that moment she longed for her dear friend—the only person on earth who knew and understood the real her.

Isaiah followed Addie down the bleacher steps and back onto the field. Frustrated that he didn't see her point of view at all, she just wanted the day to end so she could call Monica. She and Isaiah completed the afternoon games, but both were quiet and contemplative. Neither had much to say. They didn't win anything else either. Neither seemed to have the drive. He did try to revive the enthusiasm, but to no avail.

The minute the bus stopped in front of the gym, Adelaide stood, ready for this day to end. Isaiah offered to walk her to her dorm, but she passed. After all, his car was right there. Their thoroughbred disagreement lingered for her but seemed long past for him. Why were men like that? How did they move on so quickly? Adelaide shut her front door and pressed 3 on her speed dial, asking Monica those very questions.

"I just saw a video speaking to that matter. Men compartmentalize. Women see the whole picture. For Isaiah, the discussion was over, and he switched to his game-playing competitive compartment. I know Steve is that way. For you, it's not that easy because you don't live in compartments, you live on the whole playing field of life. That is why men can have sex fifteen minutes after a big fight that hasn't been resolved. For women, the fight is still right there, making sex nearly impossible."

"So he shifted gears." She paced around her small living room.

"And you didn't. Now what's this all about? Do you have a new man in your life that you failed to tell me about?"

"No new man, I promise. After Harold, another man holds little appeal—at least most of the time, but today for just a little while I thought Isaiah Shepherd just might make it past the no-men-allowed zone." She curled up on the wicker settee, drawing her knees up to her chest.

"Do tell."

She filled Monica in on the events of her day. "Am I so close-minded that I can't be friends with someone who has another opinion than mine? I mean, friends don't always see eye to eye on everything, do they? I need you to tell me the truth on this one—even if it will hurt."

"Okay," Monica began in her slow, contemplative way. "I think your stance on gambling is—extreme."

"But—" Adelaide wanted to defend herself.

"Wait. Let me finish. You wanted the truth."

"You're right. I'm sorry. Not another word." Wanting the truth and actually hearing it were two different things.

"I do understand why you feel as strongly as you do. Gambling devastated your life—of course you hate it. But you're coming at it from an unusual place. It's touched you in a way most of us have never experienced. Just like a mom whose child was killed by a drunk driver would have extreme feelings about drinking and driving. But she can't stop all people from owning cars."

Adelaide's heart hardened against the words, but she heard the truth in them, too. This time even Monica didn't seem to really get it.

"What if that mom came to you and accused you of an atrocity because you own a car? Don't you think you'd feel a little like Isaiah did today?"

"I guess. It just seems different."

"Because it's not personal to you, Adelaide. Horse racing is."

"Thank you for the truth. Pray for me to really 'get it.' I don't want to be close-minded."

"As God heals your heart, I think the issues will clear up. As for the friends part, there are things we don't see eye to eye on, and yet we're best buds. And for how many years now?"

"You're right, of course, and how long has it been? Shortly after I moved to Dallas."

"Jen was a baby. I hadn't had the two boys yet. When did we take that Navigators 2:7 course?"

"It was about twenty-five years ago." Adelaide felt amazed by the revelation.

"Three years in intensive Bible study bonds people. Even people who don't agree on everything. Now go out and make friends with that handsome hunk. He sounds yummy."

"He is. Everything about him is perfect, except the horse issue and the fact that we work together. No romances between coworkers."

"That makes him all the safer, since you aren't looking for a romance, just a buddy."

"You're right. I should have seen it that way. I don't have to worry about the pressure to date since I never plan to do that ever again. Monica, thanks so much for speaking truth. I miss you. Come visit me soon." Not for the first time, Adelaide thanked God for her dear friend.

&

A couple of weeks passed, and Isaiah had only seen Adelaide in class. She always had a smile for him, but that was their only interaction. He glanced out the window of his office. The fall semester was in full swing. Maybe he'd call her and see if she wanted to join him for a football game and a burger. They could use the certificate they won. He wasn't certain she'd agree. She held some pretty strong opinions about his horses. Who in her life had a gambling problem? It was obviously a very personal topic to her.

"You have a minute?" James asked as he rapped on Isaiah's open door.

Isaiah turned his chair to face forward, and James took a seat across the desk from him.

"How are things going?"

"Good. You?" Isaiah knew James had something on his mind. He never just dropped by for a chat like Walt might.

"I have some concerns." James cleared his throat. The kids often referred to him as the Drama King.

Figures. Isaiah said nothing and waited for James to make some great proclamation.

"Adelaide English—how is she doing?"

Isaiah knew sooner or later James would take issue with something Addie was or wasn't doing. "She's fine. Why?" In truth, Isaiah had been remiss in meeting with her weekly. When their relationship got personal, he stepped back. Unprofessional? Yep. Now he knew why they asked staff to keep relationships platonic. He'd remedy that as soon as James was finished with his inquiry.

"Fine? Really?" James lifted one brow. The man was intense.

Isaiah decided to quit beating around the bush. "What are you getting at, James?"

"There are rumors."

Isaiah nodded. "Always are."

"I've gotten several negative reports regarding one of her RAs and what she's doing in Zion Hall."

"Such as?" Isaiah's patience grew thin.

"Drinking, sex, breaking curfew. You name it."

Isaiah rose. "I'll look into it." He moved around his desk. "I haven't heard any of that, though. You'd think I'd know."

James rose. "You'd think."

They walked out into the hall together, pausing before heading two different directions. "I'd like a full report within the week."

"You've got it. See you later." Isaiah turned and headed for the front doors, sighing. He didn't have time for this right now, especially since the chance of any truth in the rumors was slim to none. However, this provided the perfect excuse to see Addie again. He smiled at the prospect.

Minutes later he stood outside her front door, knocking. The door swung open, and surprise etched itself across her features when she discovered him standing there. "Isaiah."

"We haven't had our weekly meeting the past couple of weeks, nor have we met for coffee or dinner as we agreed, so what do you say—dinner out, the football game, and coffee afterward? That will take care of it all in one fell swoop."

"Sure."

Now he was surprised. "I'll pick you up at five." He hadn't expected her to respond so quickly or easily.

"See you then."

That was painless, and he had himself a date. Well, not a date per se, but plans with a "friend." He'd have to work at thinking of her in that way. She was way too much woman for a friend.

❧

"What should I wear?" Adelaide had called Lissa for advice.

"Wear those cute designer jeans I sent you, a sweater, and a pair of boots. Your UGGs would be perfect."

Adelaide rummaged through her closet and dragged out the prescribed items. "Got 'em. Thanks."

"Mom, is this a date?"

"No, nothing like that. We're just combining our meeting with some fun."

"Hmm."

"No really. Not a date." Adelaide pulled on the jeans while holding the phone on one shoulder.

"I know you could never date Mr. Almost Perfect because he has that one flaw—he raises horses."

"Not horses—thoroughbreds." She snapped and zippered the jeans. "I think these are tighter on me than they were on you."

"If they are, I'm sure it's not by much. We're very close in size. All my friends' moms secretly hate you."

"Yeah, right. Hey, I've got to run. He'll be here in five."

Isaiah arrived right on time, looking great. Tonight instead of an oxford shirt, he wore a college sweatshirt. He opened the car door, and she settled into his little Mazda Miata. "I figured you for a pickup."

"And I have one. My sons and I share this car for special occasions. Since they're both away at college, I've got full rights." He sent a smile her direction that messed with her insides.

"Lucky you. Where do your sons attend college?"

"My oldest, Nathaniel, is in Seattle at U-Dub."

"U-Dub?"

"University of Washington. He's a senior, and Jonathan is a sophomore at Azusa Pacific, where Julie and I went. He really misses his mom, and I think he hopes to feel a connection with her there."

Isaiah pulled up next to the green clapboard building. The parking lot was almost full.

"Have you been here yet?" He turned off the engine.

"No." She unbuckled her seat belt.

"It's a local favorite."

They both climbed out, and he held open the glass door to the grill for her. The walls jumped out at her. The bottom half were paneled, and the top half were painted kelly green and covered with baseball memorabilia.

"You a fan?" he asked. They followed the hostess to a booth.

"Not so much." She settled onto her bench seat and opened the menu.

"I figured you weren't, but you've had a few surprises for me. Thought baseball might be another."

"Nope. Sorry. What do you recommend?"

"They have great pizza, good burgers—everything, really."

She turned the menu over. "Wow, this started as a gas station in 1921."

"And it has been reinvented several times since."

His word choice surprised her—*reinvented*. Did he somehow know that's what she was doing? *Will the new and improved—reinvented—version of Adelaide English please rise?* Sometimes she had no idea who she was. First she'd succumbed to her dad's demands and then Harold's. Who was the real Adelaide English? What was she even like? Close-minded? Unapproachable? Fearful? Or maybe grace-filled, warm, and brave?

seven

After church on Sunday, Adelaide announced a dinner with her ten RAs for Monday evening. They'd been meeting together regularly, but she still didn't know any of them well, except Robin. Isaiah challenged her to work harder at getting to know them.

After the dinner was set, she called Monica. "Those girls must think I'm too old to be their friend. I have to work harder at proving them wrong. I'm just not sure how to make friends with someone who's uninterested. Lissa and I are good friends, but she tells me most of her friends keep their parents at a distance. You're good friends with your kids."

"Thankfully I am, but most kids are like that these days," Monica commiserated. "Our society as a whole paints anything middle-aged and beyond as archaic and unnecessary."

"No wonder they look at me like I have two heads." She let out a disgusted sound. "I've been trying to mother them."

"Maybe mothering them isn't the right approach." She could picture the concern in Monica's expression, even though two thousand miles separated them.

"But what approach works? The mothering approach has always served me well with Lissa's friends—even the guys."

"But they expected you to be just another mom. These kids left home and their moms far behind. They probably don't want to find another 'mom' waiting for them at college." Monica's wisdom never failed to make sense.

"You're right, of course. The problem is that Dr. James

Dunlap didn't like me from the beginning. I'm sure he'd love to see me go, and he's apparently been checking up on me. Now he wants a full report from Isaiah. How do you write a report on relationships? I mean, they are nice girls, but we are far from buds."

"What about Isaiah? Where does he stand on this?"

"He stated and restated his confidence in me. If only I had that much in myself."

"Well, I'm glad he's on your side."

She thought back to their night together. "Honestly, he's a stand-up guy on every front." She paused, remembering. "Of course, that's what most people thought about Harold."

"Not everyone," Monica reminded her.

"And Dr. Dunlap trumps Isaiah."

"We'll just pray." That was always Monica's answer, but it wasn't a pat answer. She was a sincere woman of faith, trusting the Lord in any and all situations. "He opened this door for you, and He is much bigger than Dr. Dunlap. Trust Him, Addie. Watch Him work."

"You're right, of course. And will you pray for me? I need to build deeper relationships. I've spent my life avoiding deep. I don't even know if I can change."

"You can't." She spoke softly, firmly. "But God can. Take it to Him a hundred times a day if that's what it takes. He'll enable you. He didn't put you there to leave you high and dry."

"I always feel better after we chat. Thank you. Pray tomorrow night at seven."

"Will do. Love you, friend."

The following evening ten girls gathered in Adelaide's apartment. They sat on her floor, her furniture, and even her coffee table. Her little living room overflowed with bodies. As she looked into each face, she asked God for a love for each of them—His supernatural love.

"I guess we've been remiss in growing together as a team, so plan on making a habit of this. We'll have a monthly dinner just to chitchat and stay in touch on a personal level."

Nobody said anything except Heather. "That will be nice."

"I hope so. Anyway, Dr. Dunlap has received some negative reports regarding us."

"Like what?" Kim asked.

"Like drinking, missing curfew, even sex in the dorm rooms." Adelaide searched each face, praying for discernment.

"No way," Milla spoke up. She was a music major and spent most of her time in the choir room.

"Look, I'm not accusing anyone. I'm just saying the accusations have been made. It's our job to either prove or disprove their validity. I'm asking each of you to make it your business to know what's happening in each of your girls' lives. Just as it's my business to know what's happening in yours." Was she sounding too mom-like?

"Fair enough," Heather said. "We can do this, girls. It's the reason we get a tuition break. Our jobs are to uphold the rules of the dorms—even if we don't agree with all of them." Heather's gaze traveled over each RA and ended on Adelaide. "I don't think those things have happened on my wing, but I'll do my best detective work to make certain they won't."

"Thank you, Heather, and thanks to each of you for your cooperation." As Adelaide's gaze roamed over each face, she worried about Erin. Her demeanor and attitude seemed unwilling to cooperate. She'd watch her with extra scrutiny.

"Anything else?" Kim glanced at her watch. "I have my first big exam tomorrow at eight a.m. and need some study time. Actually, I need about a week." Everyone snickered. "So if we could head to dinner now, that would be great."

"Not a problem. Let me close in prayer, and we'll head out." She'd never liked to pray aloud, except with Monica, but as their leader, she forced herself to lead. She kept the prayer short and sweet, asking for wisdom and blessing for each of them.

She'd signed out a van, so they all piled in. They had a nice time laughing, talking, and eating pizza. Robin said little, but she was naturally shy. To be honest, Addie watched and listened much more than she spoke. Erin didn't engage either. Adelaide's concern grew. She'd not pegged her as an introvert.

When they got back to the college, most of them were out the van door seconds after she parked, but Heather lingered. "Can we talk?" she asked as soon as all the other girls were gone.

"Sure." Adelaide led Heather back to her apartment and settled into her wicker chair, propping her feet on the pillow-covered ottoman, exhausted. She, too, needed some study time, but this was more important.

"I've seen Erin and Tina smoking down by the river. I've also seen them with beer in the parking lot. And boys are up and down that hall way past curfew. I don't want to be the tattletale, but thought you should know. Especially in light of the rumors. I'm afraid at least some of them are true."

"I do appreciate your telling me. I will check into it. Thanks."

Heather stood to leave, and Adelaide closed the door behind her. She leaned against it—dog tired and out of her league. She wanted to close her eyes to the truth and avoid confrontation. Had she naively assumed that Christian kids were always honest and forthright?

Failure to confront was a pattern in her life. Maybe it was

a pattern God wanted to break. The knot tightening in her stomach was a reminder that she'd never faced her suspicions regarding Harold. She knew something was going on but closed her eyes, avoiding calling him out. Maybe if she had, he'd not have spent every penny and left her owing hundreds of thousands of dollars.

❧

"Hey, thanks for meeting me for breakfast." Isaiah pulled his chair up to the table where Walt waited.

"Are you kidding? I never turn down Michael D's. Best breakfast in town. What's up?"

"Adelaide." He leaned back as the waitress poured coffee into his upturned cup.

"Adelaide? Is there a problem?" Walt moved his cup toward the waitress, and she topped it off.

They both placed their orders, and she retreated with the menus.

"James is hot on her trail." He added one packet of sugar to his coffee.

"I'm not surprised. He has that pit-bull quality when something bugs him. What's he got between his teeth this time?"

"He claims some of the girls in the freshmen dorm are breaking some pretty serious rules." Isaiah finished stirring his coffee and laid down his spoon.

"Do you think it's true?"

"I don't know." Isaiah sighed. "Maybe James was right. Maybe she can't handle the job."

"That's not like you, Zay. You never give up on people." Walt's brows creased.

"What if I made a mistake? She avoids conflict, isn't a strong leader, and hasn't built much relationship with any of the girls that I can see. I mean, I see her trying, but they aren't reciprocating."

"I don't think hiring her was a mistake, but if it was, it won't be the first or the last. You and I both felt God's leading in hiring Adelaide. Maybe there's something He wants to do in her, and she's not relinquishing yet. I'll join you in praying specifically for God's answer."

"I know He's not through with any of us yet."

"And sometimes if we're not cooperating, our disobedience clogs the system and affects a lot more than just us. My guess is, God's got big plans for her."

The waitress dropped off their plates. Walt gave thanks for the meal.

"Amen," Isaiah echoed. He placed the napkin in his lap.

"Can you come alongside her—guide and teach her?"

He was already battling internally. His attraction was growing. How could he keep her at a safe distance and invest in her life? "I've considered it."

"But?" Walt studied him.

Isaiah fought the urge to squirm under the scrutiny.

"Are you falling for her?" Walt laid his fork on his plate.

Isaiah decided to come clean. If he confessed his struggle, Walt could pray and offer some accountability. "There is a distinct possibility of that happening. She's on my mind a lot. I want her free instead of being so bound by fear and propriety. I want her to find herself—the woman God created her to be. God did that for me, and I want Him to do it for her."

"All worthy goals." Walt sipped his coffee.

"Every time I'm around her, my feelings grow stronger. Yet, we are so different. And it's all a moot point because as long as we both work here, nothing can happen."

"I don't mean to sound heartless, but feelings are just feelings. You don't have to act on them. Keep giving them to the Lord and taking captive your thoughts."

"You're right, of course. How many times have I told a student feelings come and go like the wind? And in reality, we could never make a go of a relationship—too many obstacles." But a part of his heart would sure like to try.

❧

Adelaide unlocked her door, balancing the grocery bag on one hip. She flipped on the light switch and pushed the door almost shut with her hip. Glancing at the clock above her kitchen sink, she set her bag and purse on the tiny table for two that graced one corner of the equally small kitchen. Almost midnight. No wonder she was beyond tired.

She returned to the living room to lock the front door. A piece of paper lay on the tile floor just inside the doorway. Upon closer inspection, it was a note printed in nondescript handwriting in black ink. "Erin's having sex in her room right now." Adelaide wanted to cry. Not only was she tired, she didn't want to deal with this now—or ever, if she was honest.

Grabbing her pint of milk from the still-full grocery bag, she shoved it in the fridge. Then she snatched her keys from the table and headed down the hall toward Erin's wing. "What do I do, Lord?" This situation was beyond her. She knocked on Erin's door, but of course no one answered. Glancing down at the keys in her hand, she remembered the master key. Did she have the guts to walk in unannounced?

She'd wait in the hall. How could she just barge in? It went against everything in her. Besides, what sort of scene might she stumble into? She moved a couple of doors down and lowered herself to the floor. She was liking jeans more and more. Pulling her knees to her chest, she folded her arms across them, resting her head on her forearms.

The hall was now quiet and dimly lit. Curfew on weeknights was twelve, so by now there weren't too many milling around. Occasionally a girl or two walked by, but most everyone appeared to be in their rooms for the evening. She got a few smiles or nods, but no one stopped to talk. That was a relief. What would she say?

Maybe Erin's "friend" had already left. Was this a complete waste of time? Before long, she struggled to stay awake. What would Isaiah do? She had no idea, but this seemed futile. An hour passed. She dozed off and on. Then another hour.

She stood and stretched, her limbs cramped and stiff. Face it, this could be a hoax. Or he could slip out the window or stay all night. She had a class first thing tomorrow, which was now today. Why did she think she could do this stupid job? *I'm going home.* Right choice, wrong choice, it didn't matter.

Then she heard it. Holding her breath and standing very still, she waited. A head popped out of Erin's room, glancing both ways. She pressed herself close against the wall, praying he'd not notice her. She was glad she was on the same side of the hall as Erin's room. She was less likely to be seen than if she were across from him.

Sure enough, he stepped from the room, heading down the hall. Then he saw her. He stopped. Adelaide's heart pounded. He pulled his cap down low and ran past her. In the low lighting, she'd never be able to recognize him again. She quickly went to Erin's door and knocked softly before the guy had a chance to warn her.

Erin swung the door open. "You forget some—" She stopped. She tried to cover her scantily clad body with her arms. "Mrs. E." Just then Erin's cell phone rang.

"Ignore it." Adelaide sounded tougher than she felt. "We

need to talk." She marched into the dorm room, uninvited, and closed the door, then leaned against it. Her heart pounded, the rhythm echoing in her ears.

Erin grabbed a thick robe off the floor and slipped it on, keeping her back to Adelaide. She pulled the belt tight around her petite waist. When she turned to face Adelaide, she held the top of the robe tightly closed at the neck. Silent tears streaked her face with mascara.

"Please don't report me. I'll never do it again."

Adelaide's heart went out to her. "Who is the boy?"

"Jason Stanwick. We're getting married." She sniffed.

Adelaide's gaze went to the girl's left hand, but there was no ring.

"It's not official yet. My parents would freak if I were engaged before I graduated from college. But he'll get me a ring in June just as soon as we're done here. We've dated a long time, and it's hard to keep waiting. We messed up. Please give us a second chance. Jason's on the soccer team. If you report us, he'll lose his scholarship and not be able to play his senior year."

You should have thought of that before. Her dad's voice in her memory reprimanded her for something far less life changing.

"His family is poor. Without his scholarship, he won't be able to finish school. Please don't do that to him." The silent tears turned to sobs.

Adelaide closed her eyes, leaning her head against the door. Didn't she have an obligation to apprise the school of the situation? Yet she didn't want to be as unbending as her father. Sometimes people did need a second chance.

"I don't know, Erin."

The girl slumped down onto the floor, her sobs turning

to broken wails, almost resembling a dying animal. It tore at Adelaide's heart. Finally, Erin raised her head. Black streaks smeared her face. "My father's a pastor of a very large, very conservative church. He will disown me."

"Erin, parents forgive." Well, most parents. *My dad certainly would have disowned me for such a deed, but that was a long time ago. Times have changed. It's less surprising nowadays if a couple falls. It doesn't make it right, but surely as a pastor, the man understands grace.*

"I know I'm putting you in an unfair position, but the cost to both Jason and me would be great. And the public humiliation would be more than I could bear. Please, Mrs. E., please. We'll do whatever you ask. Just please don't report us."

She wanted to let it go. She really did. She knew what having a harsh dad felt like, a dad who had no room for anything but perfection. But what would Isaiah say? He'd be so disappointed in her. And God, what would God say? *Go and sin no more.* That was what Jesus said to the woman at the well. Was God telling her to give them a second chance?

"I'm going to sleep on this, Erin. I want to meet with both you and Jason tomorrow at noon in my apartment. I'll let you know my decision then."

Sleep—ha. That was a joke.

eight

Adelaide ushered Jason and Erin into her apartment. Erin settled on the settee, and Jason took the wicker chair. Adelaide leaned against her door, saying nothing. She studied each of their faces. Sorrow clouded their eyes. The heaviness of their situation weighed on her. She wanted to do what was right for them, for the college, and for the Lord. But what was that?

Jason leaned forward, arms on his thighs, his hands clasped, his head hanging low.

Adelaide took a deep breath, trying to calm her own emotions. She'd read and reread the manual. The policy was so clear, leaving no room for error. No room for sin. No room for forgiveness. Automatic expulsion. So much like her own father. How she'd longed for a little mercy during her own growing-up years. How she'd longed for a little mercy in her marriage. Wasn't that what Christianity was all about?

Erin's gaze met hers. The girl looked so fragile. Her face, devoid of makeup, appeared pale except for the red, puffy eyes and the Rudolph-like nose. Her eyes begged Adelaide for the elusive gift of mercy.

She had to look away, fighting hard not to break into tears herself. What if this was Lissa? God forbid, but what if it was? How would she want her own daughter treated? By the letter of the law or with God's tender grace?

Jason sat up straight and cleared his throat. "Mrs. English, we made a mistake, and for that, we're truly sorry. If you can overlook this just once, we promise it will never happen again. I won't ever go into Erin's room, nor she into mine. We've learned our lesson." He reached out his hand and took Erin's, giving it a little squeeze.

He really does love her. That thought comforted Adelaide. At least it wasn't just sex for the sake of sex. The two of them crossed a line because they had deep feelings for one another. *Am I justifying sin?* Maybe. Adelaide had so many conflicting thoughts and feelings shooting through her, she had no idea how to handle this. But did she have it in her to destroy the future of these two people?

"Will you promise me that you'll never be alone together again?"

They glanced at each other and both nodded.

"We can do that," Jason promised.

"Will you meet with me once a week?" At least that would provide them some sort of accountability.

"Sure," they answered in unison. Another good sign. They were both on the same page.

"Okay, I think you're both sincerely sorry, so this one time you get a get-out-of-jail-free card." A wave of uncertainty washed over Adelaide. Was she making a huge mistake?

She swallowed away the doubt. This was the way Jesus did business. *Go and sin no more.*

"Really?" Astonishment settled on Erin's face. She jumped up and ran to where Adelaide still stood by the front door. She wrapped her arms around Adelaide, squeezing tight. "Thank you so much. You won't be sorry, I promise."

Jason stood and shook her hand. "Thanks, Mrs. E. I owe you big-time. Without your intervention, I wouldn't be able to finish school. I'll never forget you for this."

Adelaide smiled, vacillating between misgiving and complete confidence.

"You don't need to remember me, but please remember God's undeserved favor in this situation. I hope you've both repented before Him, and I hope when you leave here, you'll spend some time on your knees thanking Him. He wants us to learn from our mistakes, and there is a big difference between being sorry for the act and being sorry you got caught."

Their eyes had both sort of glazed over, and she realized she was lecturing. Lissa hated it when she shifted into that mode.

"I'm sorry. I didn't mean to preach, but I'm sort of putting myself on the line for you two."

"And we appreciate it," Jason assured her.

The three of them stood in awkward silence by her front door.

"Well, I guess you can leave. Let's meet next week—same time, same place."

As they left, doubt curled in the pit of Adelaide's stomach. She'd just put her job on the line for two kids she barely knew. Was she insane?

⊱⊰

Isaiah met with Adelaide weekly, and she filled him in on the comings and goings of her RAs. He mentored her and watched with pleasure as she grew in her role as a leader. He'd taken Walt's advice and held a tight rein on his thoughts and feelings for Adelaide. That, however, never stopped the tenderness that flooded him whenever she was near—like right now. She waited for him at their usual Starbucks table for their Wednesday afternoon meeting. When he spotted her, he nearly drowned in an onslaught of tenderness.

"Hey, you. Sorry I'm late." He ignored his inclination to bend over and kiss her.

"Not a problem. I've been studying."

"The usual?"

She nodded, and he headed off to buy their hot drinks.

When he returned with their drinks, Isaiah took the seat across from her, handing her the tall vanilla latte she loved. "You look exceptionally happy today. Good news?"

"My daughter and I are meeting in Dallas next week for Thanksgiving. It'll be good to wrap these arms around her again." Her eyes were bright with excitement. "The tickets were a gift from a friend, and until yesterday Lissa and I both thought we'd be stuck in our respective dorms eating a turkey TV dinner."

"I wouldn't have let that happen. The boys and I always go to Walt and Linda's, so we'd have dragged you along, but for your sake, I'm glad you get to be with family. Nothing can beat that. So, how'd the rest of your week go?"

"I got an A on my last test, and I'm finally making some headway with my girls. They are starting to come to me with problems, and every once in a while they actually drop by just to chat. Can you believe it?" Her eyes danced, and her cheeks were flushed from the cold weather. She had no idea what a picture she presented.

"That's wonderful." His heart overflowed with warmth.

"Thanks so much. None of this would be happening if you hadn't come alongside me these past couple of months."

"Just doing my job," he assured her. *Thank You, Lord. She's come so far.*

"I know it was more than that. Your job isn't to babysit me."

He winked but said nothing.

"Are you going to the big bonfire event on Friday night?" Adelaide wondered aloud.

"I think so. I honestly haven't given it much thought."

"Maybe I'll see you there, then." She rose and slipped her purse strap onto her shoulder. "I've got a study group in ten minutes. Sorry to cut you short, but it was the only time we could all make it. I hope you don't mind."

"Not at all."

As she moved toward the door, emptiness hit him. He wondered what she'd feel like in his arms—soft, feminine, right. *Don't go there, buddy. Do not go there.* He decided to skip the bonfire—Addie, a fire, a parade of stars in the sky above, and the cool night air spelled trouble with a capital *T.* Nope, why torture himself?

꙰

Monica met Adelaide and Lissa at the Dallas airport the following Wednesday. Lissa's plane had arrived an hour before Adelaide's, so they were waiting in baggage claim. Spotting them the minute she stepped off the escalator, she rushed toward them. They were talking and hadn't noticed her approach. Out of nowhere, a lump clogged her throat. Her daughter and her closest—sort of, only—friend. The two most precious people in the world to her were only seconds away from her embrace. How she'd missed them both—it had been more than three months since she'd seen either.

"Mom!" Lissa jumped up and hugged her.

Monica followed suit, and the three of them held on to each other for a very long time. Adelaide heard each of them sniffle at least once, so she knew some of the same emotions that hit her had affected them as well.

"You have no idea how good it is to be here." Adelaide dried her damp cheeks with her fingers. She gave Monica another hug. "Thanks so much. Flying us both here was much too generous." She grabbed Lissa's hand. "You and Steve have hearts of gold."

"Or an ulterior motive. I selfishly wanted to see you." Her grin lit her whole face. "I'm so glad you're home."

"Mom, is that your suitcase?" Lissa headed to the belt that carried every size, shape, and color of luggage imaginable. She returned with Adelaide's designer bag.

Lissa towed her bag and Adelaide's as they followed Monica out of the airport. Once they had the bags loaded and were buckled in the car, Adelaide turned around and faced Lissa in the backseat. "Are you adjusting to being poor?"

She shrugged. "I admit that sometimes it's hard."

"I know. I still have the expensive clothes, shoes, and handbags, but yet I can't afford my own plane ticket. Most people at school just assume I'm wealthy. Little do they know, I've never been so broke in my entire life. I have to limit myself to only two Starbucks a week."

At that moment, Monica pulled into the Starbucks drive-through.

"I wasn't hinting." Adelaide quickly pulled out her wallet. "At least let me treat."

"Nope." Lissa's one word had an authoritative ring to it. "Remember, I said I had a surprise for you when we got to Dallas? Well, this is it. I got a job at Starbucks, so it's my treat. I get a great discount."

"Honey, aren't you already working part-time for the college?"

"Yeah, but it's only fifteen hours a week."

Monica pulled a little past the window, so Lissa could give them her employee number and settle the bill.

"And how many hours are you working at Starbucks?" Concern added an edge to her tone.

"Around ten or fifteen. I just needed some fun money so I can afford the coffee addiction my mom passed on to me."

"But what about your grades?" Her intense feelings toward Harold rose to the forefront once more. Every time she thought she'd made progress, the anger resurfaced. *I hate that you've ruined her senior year, Harold. I hate what you've done to us. Then you up and die, and we have to clean up your mess.* Her clenched fists were the only outward sign of her inward struggle. She longed to scream her hatred at the top of her lungs. Instead she accepted her hot vanilla latte with a smile.

"I'm sorry, Mom, what did you ask?"

"Your grades? Can you keep them up and work that much?"

"Yep. I'll be fine, I promise. Hey, Monica, would you mind dropping me off at Reese's? She got home from Grove City today, and Mom said she'd give me up for a few hours to visit my best friend. That will give you two some girl time as well."

"Don't mind at all. Is she the one who lives right around the corner from your old house?"

"She does."

When Monica turned into their old neighborhood, more anger rose. Adelaide tried to force her gaze to stay trained on the pavement, but she had to look up as they passed their old house. An expensive sports car sat in the circle drive. "They painted." She'd hoped to sound casual, but the two words were steeped in sadness.

"It's hard to imagine another family living there." Lissa's soft words tore at Adelaide's heart.

Monica rounded a corner.

"The Bordners are the second house on the left." Lissa climbed from the car and went around to the front passenger door. She pulled the door open and hugged Adelaide. "I'll have Reese give me a ride home. Would about nine tonight be okay?"

"Sure, hon." She kissed her daughter's cheek, and Lissa shut the door.

Monica waited until Lissa disappeared into the house. Then she focused on Adelaide. "You okay?"

"No. So many emotions have slammed me since arriving back in Texas." She looked directly into Monica's blue eyes. "I hate Harold. I hate him. And I cannot even believe I'm saying those words aloud, but I do. And it's growing more intense."

"I understand. Some days I don't like Harold much either." She pulled away from the curb. "Do you want to go somewhere to talk?"

"Your kitchen table is perfect. Is Steve home?"

Monica glanced at her watch. "We have a few hours until he gets off."

Monica lived only about a mile from their old neighborhood. "We'll leave the bags, and Steve can carry them in when he gets home from work. That will give us more uninterrupted talk time."

"It feels so good to be in your kitchen once again," Adelaide commented as they entered from the garage. She settled into a chair at the round table in the window nook. "Almost like home."

Monica grabbed the chair next to Adelaide. "I'm glad we have these few hours without your daughter and my husband."

"I have this brand-new life, which Lissa refers to as my second chance. An opportunity to reinvent myself. I know I should be grateful, and don't get me wrong, I am. I thank God every day for the job and the opportunity, but I miss you and Dallas and. . .money. There, I said it. Am I horrible?"

Monica shook her head. "No. I'd say you're normal. You

lived a pretty nice life. And now you live in a college dorm—paycheck to paycheck. Big change. And you're grieving—not just Harold, but everything familiar."

"How do I get through it? I mean, I know all the trite answers, but when the rubber of my life meets the road of faith, how do I walk through this in a way that honors God? I feel like I'm going backward. My bitterness toward Harold is growing daily. How do I deal with it?"

Monica stared at her Starbucks cup, twisting it in her hands. "Day by day—praying, reading the Word, taking captive your thoughts. All the trite answers that you already know."

"Why does it sound so much easier than it is?"

"Because God wants us to know Him through the tough seasons. If all our victories were won in a few days, we'd have little need for God."

"You're always so wise."

"You haven't mentioned Isaiah. Anything new with him?"

His name always lightened her heavy heart. "He's my if-only."

"If-only?"

"You know, if only I hadn't made a million mistakes, I'd love to have a man like him. If only I'd met him instead of Harold all those years ago. If only. . ." She paused. "I'd love for you to meet him someday. He's this great guy—kind, macho, not polished like Harold, but pretty wonderful." She knew she was saying too much, but with Monica her heart always poured out like an open book.

"Sounds pretty good to me. You know, you're allowed to move on. Harold's been gone almost a year and a half."

Adelaide sighed. "Not with this one, I'm not. A, he's my boss and dating coworkers isn't permitted. B, I'm not at all his type, and C, it's only a crush. You know, admiration from afar. He's smart and has this passionate love for Jesus. You should hear him teach. He's amazing and kind. Other than your Steve, I don't know many kind men."

"I know. Maybe that's why I wish you'd take this great guy a little more seriously. Who knows, Addie, maybe he's the whole reason you're in Idaho. Why don't you pray about it?"

"I don't know that my heart can take much more disappointment." Tears hovered nearby.

Monica patted her hand. "Maybe someday."

"You know, he calls me Addie, too. And do you want to know the best thing about him?" Talking about him brought a smile to her lips. "He's so free."

"What do you mean?"

"He's just himself. Doesn't care what anyone thinks as long as God is pleased with him. I'd give anything to be so uninhibited. I honestly don't even know who I really am. I've spent my life trying to keep peace and be the person first that my dad expected and then Harold. Who am I?" Those pesky tears returned, and this time a stubborn one made it down her cheek.

"You and God will figure that out. Keep asking, and sooner or later you'll know."

"Too much later, and I'll be too old to care."

Monica chuckled. "Finally, your dry wit returns."

Adelaide's cell phone rang. "That's weird. It's Erin. I'd better get this. She's one of my RAs." She flipped open the phone and rose from the table, walking into the kitchen. "Hello?"

"I'm pregnant." Erin cried so hard Adelaide barely understood the words.

Shock reverberated through her. "No," she whispered, unable to find her voice.

"My dad's coming after you and Jason. I thought I should let you know."

Adelaide heard a click. "Erin? Erin, are you there? Erin?" She closed her phone, and the gesture felt as final as the end of her tenure at the Lord's College. She closed her eyes and hung her head. How would her poor decision affect Isaiah? What would he think of her now?

nine

Isaiah glanced at the caller ID on his ringing cell phone. "Adelaide?" *Why is she calling me on Sunday evening?*

"I'm so sorry to bother you at home on the weekend, but I just flew in from Dallas. Something concerning has happened. Can we meet before class tomorrow?"

"Are you all right?" *What could be so pressing?*

"Yes. . . No. . . I don't know. I just. . .I need to talk to you before the day gets rolling tomorrow."

"My office at seven?"

"I'll be there. Thank you." And the call ended.

He lowered the phone from his ear and stared at it for several seconds. He tried to let the conversation go and forget about it until tomorrow, but he found his mind playing twenty questions.

The following morning, he arrived at his office about fifteen minutes early, just in case Adelaide showed up before their scheduled time. And he'd guessed right. About ten till, she walked through his door. He knew instantly that something bad had happened. Her pale, drawn face caused his heart to constrict.

"May I shut this?" She gestured toward the door. "I know it goes against school policy, but this is a private matter that I don't want to have overheard."

He nodded. "Just leave it open an inch or so."

She perched on the edge of the upholstered chair facing him. Her large eyes reflected fear.

Say it, Addie. Just say it.

She sucked in a deep breath. "Erin is pregnant."

"Erin Martin?"

Addie nodded.

"I'm sad to hear that. How far along?"

"I don't know. I really know very little—except her father is coming after me and the boy."

"You? That's ridiculous. Don't worry, we have a group of Christian lawyers on retainer for such a time as this." Isaiah jotted a note to call them as soon as this meeting ended.

"I knew."

He barely caught the quietly uttered words. What was she saying? He waited. Her gaze was lowered, so he couldn't see her eyes. "What do you mean you knew?"

"Six or eight weeks ago I discovered she was sexually active."

"Here? On campus?"

"In her dorm."

"And you did nothing?" He rubbed the back of his neck. *Oh, Adelaide.*

"Not nothing exactly." She filled him in on the events that had transpired some weeks ago. "They haven't been together in that way again since."

Torn between her compassionate way of handling the situation and the school's policy, he said nothing.

"She called while I was in Dallas and said her dad wants my head on a platter. That's not an exact quote, but the gist of the conversation nonetheless."

"So this won't be a quiet affair." He leaned back in his chair, thinking. "I assume the guy is Jason Stanwick?"

Addie nodded. "How did you know?"

"I see them together all the time. They've been dating since freshman year. That length of time can be a dangerous thing. Some couples make it without falling; most don't."

He pondered the information. *What is the best way to handle this?* He had to be honest with Addie and prepare her for what might be coming.

"You understand by going around policy, you've put your job at risk?"

She nodded. Her bottom lip quivered.

He rose from his chair and paced across the room. "I don't want to fire you, but I may not have a choice." He faced her, praying he'd not be forced into that, but with James it was possible.

"I'm a people pleaser." Her voice quaked with emotion. "This is a life pattern for me. I avoid confrontation and end up paying a high price in the end because I try to keep the whole world happy." She hung her head. "I feel horrible that I've put you in a bad position. Please forgive me, Isaiah."

It took all his willpower not to move around the desk and wrap her in his arms. "I do forgive you. I might have been tempted to do the same thing. Who knows?"

He refocused on Addie. "I've met her dad on several occasions. You do realize who he is, don't you?"

"The big TV preacher from Oklahoma?"

"Megachurch. Megaman. Ultra-conservative. Powerful. Not many people tell him no." He sighed and returned to his chair. "I mean no disrespect to him, but I want you to realize what we're up against." The few times his path and Chuck Martin's had crossed, the man knew what he wanted and was determined to get it. "His church is also a large contributor to the college."

"Erin's told me a little about her dad." Addie's sad gaze met his. "I had one sort of like him."

He was caught by surprise. She rarely shared anything personal. He studied her, wishing he knew her better. Who was she—the real her buried deep inside?

"Should I resign now? I mean, would that be the best thing for the college?"

"No." He answered quickly and knew maybe it was more personal than professional. "I'll call the lawyers and meet with the board. By then I'll know how to proceed through this. In the meantime, carry on." He wanted to encourage her, but, frankly, he feared the way this might play out. Reverend Martin would probably want the blame placed squarely on Adelaide and Jason. His daughter would be the innocent victim in all this.

"Again, I can't reiterate how sorry I am. I know this is my fault. I should have come to you immediately. Thank you for forgiving me. I know I've made a mess of things for you as well."

"Not my first mess to deal with." He winked, longing to reassure her, but couldn't. Would she make it through this ordeal with a job? He doubted it. But maybe God would fill their hearts with the same grace and mercy she measured out. He was powerless to help, except for prayer, and that he'd do faithfully.

⁂

Later that same morning, Adelaide was summoned to Dr. James Dunlap's office. Her heart pounded as she read the note. She'd been called out of class. *Is this how a child feels when they are sent to the principal's office?*

His secretary sat outside his office just as Rose did Isaiah's. She'd longed to stop as she passed Isaiah's office and ask him to come with her as moral support, but she didn't want to put him in an awkward or unfair position. She rounded the corner into Dr. Dunlap's office. Uncertain she could speak, she handed the note to his administrative assistant. Her hand shook slightly, and the rustling paper only served to make it abundantly clear that she was a nervous wreck.

The lady, whose nameplate on the top of her desk said IRIS FLANNIGAN, read the handwritten scribble aloud. "Report to Dr. Dunlap's office immediately." The woman glanced over her bifocals and studied Adelaide. "I'll let him know you're here." She rose and stuck her head in the partially opened door. "Mrs. English has arrived." Then she waved the crumpled note in the air. "So this is what happens when I'm at lunch? Chicken scratch." She shook her head and faced Adelaide. "Go right in."

Adelaide shot up a quick prayer as she traipsed the few steps to the inner office. She took a deep breath before pushing the door open. Her gaze met Walt's, and he sent a compassionate smile her direction. Then she spotted Isaiah next to Walt at the big conference table. His gaze touched her heart and sent her unspoken hope.

Dr. Dunlap was at the head of the table, and his eyes held accusation. He might as well have yelled from the rooftop, "I knew she couldn't do this job. Couldn't cut it, could you?" The know-it-all expression he wore made her want to scream. How did he get such a prestigious position here? His charm and warmth?

"Please come in, Mrs. English, and close the door behind you." His tone was no-nonsense, as was his erect posture.

She did as instructed.

"I assume you know why you're here?"

She nodded. Isaiah rose and pulled out the chair next to him. Grateful, she made a beeline straight for him, feeling like a bug being studied under a magnifying glass. All eyes in the room were on her. Once seated, Isaiah introduced her to several board members she'd not yet met. They were all older gentlemen. She wasn't sure if that was a good thing or a bad thing, but their age might make them as conservative as the college they oversaw.

"The reason I've gathered you all here this morning is because of a phone call I received at six a.m. today." He gazed into Adelaide's face. "I don't relish early morning calls because they are, by nature, always bad news. This one was no different. Thus the reason for the meeting."

He cleared his throat. "Chuck Martin is quite upset." He filled everyone in on the details of Erin's pregnancy. "He holds the college in general and Mrs. English in particular responsible."

Isaiah gave her hand an encouraging pat. It was on the arm of her chair, under the table, so no one but the two of them were aware of the gesture. She turned her palm up and squeezed his fingers—just to say thanks, but such tenderness shot through her that she quickly pulled her hand away. Feelings of warmth, appreciation, and unnamed emotions that she refused to explore washed over her. This man had been a rock for her since she arrived here. How grateful she was.

She refocused on James.

"Did you, in fact, break the school policy by not reporting the incident?"

"I did." She proceeded to reiterate everything that transpired from beginning to end, including her decision not to turn them in.

"Mrs. English, do I understand you to say that God told you to break the rules? God told you to send them off with a verse of scripture and barely a swat on the hand?" one of the board members addressed her. His brow creased in disbelief.

"No, sir. I didn't mean to imply that God told me to do any of this—"

"Glad we cleared that up because God doesn't lead us to break rules and disregard man's laws."

"Yes, sir. As I was saying, I and I alone am responsible for the decision. I'm not blaming God or putting this on Him in any way. I acted on my own, but I did pray. And in my heart, I believed I did the right thing for that particular situation."

"So, Mrs. English, if you had to do it again, you'd make exactly the same decision?"

I should say no, assure him that I've learned from my mistake and that nothing like that would ever happen again. But in all honesty, she couldn't. "I have no idea." Fear raced through her veins. Her heart pounded until she thought it might explode, but she had to speak up. "I, of course, believe God created sex to only be practiced within the marriage relationship. And I know beyond doubt that what they did was wrong. But they are good kids who made a bad decision. I just offered what I'd want for my daughter—a second chance, forgiveness, undeserved favor."

She heard Isaiah's quick intake of breath. The room was quiet. She wondered if every person there heard the racing of her pulse. Shocked eyes bored into her. She swallowed. "I'm sorry. I don't mean to sound critical, but what about grace? What about mercy? What about Christ's example of not casting stones? Remember the woman at the well?"

"What about keeping order, Mrs. English? What about holy living? What about being an example to the world?"

Isaiah spoke up. "And you are right on all those counts, James. But they all have to blend together somehow. It can't be all grace, all the time, nor can it be rules only, without mercy. Otherwise we become pharisaical. We have to have balance in our approach. Jesus' example should be our model."

Inside Adelaide was smiling. Isaiah had stuck up for her! And defended her. Even more important than any of that, he got it—understood how she felt and why. He might even agree! Somehow having him on her side was enough—whatever the outcome, his support was enough.

❧

James studied him intently. "This is neither the time—nor the place—to debate the rules that have been guiding us for nearly a century. We are here to address two issues, and only two. The first is Mrs. English's complete disregard for school policy. As an employee of the college, she is paid to follow the rules laid down by the men who founded this great institution. She was not hired to agree with them or change them, but to follow them."

No one could argue with what he said. Though Addie's heart had honorable intentions, she had broken the very policies they employed her to uphold. He'd hoped she would come in here with an attitude of regret, not as a maverick trying to change the world. There would be time for that later. For a people pleaser, she was bold when her beliefs were tried.

"So based on the reasons for this meeting, we are here to decide the fate of three people—Erin Martin, Jason Stanwick, and Adelaide English. That will be done according to the policies"—he held up the fat black book—"left for us by our predecessors." He turned his gaze on Adelaide. "Not our preferences, our personal belief systems, or our feelings on the subject at hand."

Adelaide nodded.

With each word uttered by James, Isaiah lost more hope for Adelaide's job to be saved. They might as well fire her and get it over with. That's where all this was heading. And on a personal level, he wasn't ready to say good-bye to her—not now and maybe not ever. The realization stunned him. He glanced her direction. Her large brown eyes focused intently on James. Her hands gripped the arms of her chair so tightly that her knuckles were white.

He had to fight for her—at least try. Otherwise Addie would be history.

"What you've done is grounds for termination." James didn't mince words.

"I understand." She drew her lips into a tight line.

"Or probation, according to article five section seven." Isaiah had spent the last few hours—between meeting with Addie and this meeting—poring over the employee handbook and refreshing his memory. He knew she'd need a well-informed ally.

James nodded. "Or possible probation. The board will make that decision this afternoon. Are there any other questions for Mrs. English before we dismiss her?"

No one responded.

"Thank you, Mrs. English, for your participation in the procedure. I hope you understand how serious this offense is. You are dismissed."

She nodded.

"We'll ask you to return at two this afternoon for the rendering of the board's final decisions."

"Yes, sir."

They all rose. "Drop by my office," Isaiah whispered near her ear.

She nodded and gave him a halfhearted smile.

He excused himself from the meeting for a brief moment. Erin waited in the outer office for her interview with the board. The girl's nose was buried in a book, and she didn't look up, so Isaiah said nothing.

Addie waited just inside the door of his office. "Rose wasn't at her desk, so I let myself in. Hope that's okay and not in the rulebook somewhere." Her frustration spilled out, and he understood.

He pushed the door almost shut. About two feet separated them. He'd asked her here to encourage her and lift her spirits, but his arms ached to pull her close. The air between them was palpable—charged with electricity. Their gazes locked, and a magnetic pull drew them together. She broke eye contact and walked to his window, putting much-needed distance between them.

"I blew it, didn't I?" She turned to face him. His desk and half the room now separated them. Safer. Much safer.

"What happened to the people pleaser?"

"I had to be honest. I don't know if I'd do it differently the next time. If I even could do it differently the next time. I wanted to lie—I did. I wanted to tell them what they wanted to hear, but ultimately would it have made a difference? Dr. Dunlap has never liked me."

Those words were true. He just didn't know if she'd realized it until now.

"I feel like I let you down—again. But as strange as it is coming from me, the principles are more important, this time, than saving me. They need to look past this incident to the policy manual. I know there are always consequences to our choices—both our bad ones and good ones. I'm not disagreeing with that. I just feel automatically expelling every student who falls into that particular sin is a strong punishment. Why is sex the unpardonable sin, but drinking, cheating, and stealing aren't? They are all the same in God's eyes." She moved from behind the desk toward the door. "Thank you, Isaiah, for everything. I feel like at least you get where I'm coming from on this." She held out her hand, but instead of offering his for a handshake, he cupped hers between the two of his.

"You are right on so many levels."

She pulled her hand from his. "Good-bye, Isaiah." Her words held finality.

His heart dipped at her words, but he managed a smile. Would she leave? At least she'd grown and changed this semester, and he felt proud of her.

ten

After lunch, Isaiah walked toward James's office. They'd finished the interviews about an hour ago and taken a break. Many emotions battled within. The one rising to the top of the heap was his intense desire to protect Addie. Tender feelings like small green shoots sprouting out of the spring-warmed earth burst forth in his heart. He wanted to know every nuance of her life, spend time with her, but most of all he yearned to wrap her in his arms and shelter her from this storm. If she lost her job, he wasn't even sure she'd finish the semester. Finances seemed to be an issue.

Walt was the only one at the table when Isaiah arrived. By his expression, Isaiah could pretty much read his thoughts. "Not looking good, is it?"

"Nope." He shook his head.

James and three of the board members entered. They'd probably lunched together. Some days Isaiah hated all the politics surrounding his job. Why did it have to be that way at a small Christian college?

When they all settled at the table, James called the meeting to order and opened with prayer. Isaiah once again asked God to intervene. Speak. Move hearts.

"Well, gentlemen. We all know the issue. Any last words before we take a vote?"

"Yes," Walt spoke up. "James, you didn't like Mrs. English from the onset. Is it possible for you to be unbiased during these proceedings?"

Whoa, way to hammer the truth home in front of the board.

James turned his gaze toward the three board members. "It's true, gentlemen. I was opposed to hiring Mrs. English due to her lack of job experience. In my opinion, she displayed no strong leadership qualities, but when it came to the vote, Dr. Shepherd and Dr. Richards banded together and had the final say."

Banded together? Isaiah didn't like the implication of James's word choice. "You skirted the question. Are you here as an unbiased board member?" *Or is this your way of saying, "I told you so"?*

"I believe so. The question is, Dr. Shepherd, are you?"

"Am I what?"

"Unbiased?" James skillfully turned the question from himself to Isaiah.

Am I? Not anymore. "I had no bias in hiring her. I felt she was our best option and still do."

"Though I didn't want to hire her, I accepted your decision and had all but forgotten it."

Had you? "I agree with everyone in this room. Mrs. English failed to carry out her job responsibilities according to our policies. I agree that no matter what her opinion is or was, she should proceed according to the directives. But this is her first offense."

"Is it? I came to you with concerns months ago." James was as determined as Isaiah.

"Those were addressed and corrected." Isaiah clenched his jaw.

"Point being, this isn't her first offense."

"She's grown into her position and is now doing a great job. She struggled early on, but has now resolved those issues. All I'm asking is that you consider probation rather than termination. Give her another chance. How many has God given each of us?"

He searched each face of the other men at the table. Other than Walt, their stony expressions appeared unmoved.

"Any other thoughts?" James asked. No one said a word. "Shall we take it to a vote?"

"Before we do, I'd like to explain my position to Isaiah." Warren was a gentle giant who'd served on this board longer than any of the rest of them. "Whether the policies are right, wrong, or in need of updating, Mrs. English is in a position of authority. Students look to her as an example, so if we let this slide this one time, what message are we sending the student body?"

"Grace?"

"When you start bending rules, chaos ensues. The lines are no longer clear. People push hard to force the boundaries further and further back. Where does it end? Rogue employees make decisions and set policies by their very behavior. I believe we must let her go, or we will be creating bigger problems for ourselves down the road."

Isaiah had sensed this was the direction they'd take, but actually hearing the thoughts spoken aloud cemented the reality. Adelaide English was about to be fired, and there wasn't a thing he could do about it. He wanted to be her hero and save the day.

"I do want to recommend, however, that we review our policies. Mrs. English made a valid point that we have left Christ out of the very core of our rules. They are, indeed— what did she say?—pharisaical."

❧

Adelaide had followed the river for a couple of miles—just thinking. Now it was time to face her accusers. Their opinion of her didn't matter nearly as much as Isaiah's did. She couldn't get him out of her mind or the near incident in his office. If she hadn't moved away from him, she'd have fallen into his arms, laid her head against his broad chest, and rested there.

What was wrong with her? Isaiah was off-limits. Yes, he'd been nice, encouraging, and sometimes when he looked at her, she felt his approval. But to be thinking about him in that way—as a man—was wrong. He'd never given her any reason for her thoughts to head in that direction, yet they did more and more often.

When she arrived at Dr. Dunlap's outer office, Iris directed her to have a seat. The door between them and the inner sanctum was shut tight. Jason and Erin were already there. She smiled at them. Erin's cold stare surprised her. How had Adelaide become the enemy? Jason gave her a slight nod. There seemed to be tension between the two of them. Sin did that. She knew it well.

The phone rang. Iris said, "Yes," into her receiver and hung up. "You may go in now." The three of them rose. Erin led the way, and Adelaide straggled behind. She rubbed her sweaty palms on the thighs of her navy pants. Isaiah's gaze caught hers. He sent her a little smile. At least he was behind her—even though she'd made his job and life tougher, he was still on her team.

She reclaimed the same chair she'd had earlier. Jason and Erin settled at the opposite end of the table from James. An extra chair had been added since she'd been in here a few hours before.

"We are a disciplinary board formed for occasions such as this. It always saddens us when we actually have to sit on a case." James made eye contact with first her and then his gaze moved to Erin and Jason. "We are here to render our decisions based on our personal interviews and the college policy book. Each member of the board has had a chance to express their opinions and concerns. They've also had the opportunity to cast a vote. A two-thirds majority vote must be rendered for an action to be implemented."

Adelaide's mouth had gone dry. Her stomach tightened with fear.

"Erin Martin, your position as an RA will be terminated, as will any and all leadership involvement. You will be required to have a roommate, no male visitors will be allowed at any time, and you will be banned from participating in any student-body activities." She sat straight and tall, nodding her head with each pronouncement. Tears pooled in her eyes, but she somehow kept them from falling. "Other than attending your classes, you'll only be allowed to participate in the graduation exercises next May."

Adelaide let out the breath she hadn't realized she was holding. It was better than she'd expected for Erin. At least she could finish her degree. A tiny seed of hope found its way into Adelaide's heart.

"Jason, we're expelling you."

Adelaide gasped, and the hope shriveled. His future was ruined. He dropped his head so she could no longer see his face. His shoulders drooped with the weight of the news. The strange thing was, Erin didn't seem surprised, nor did she glance his direction. What happened to the deep love they'd proclaimed? Sin had a way of stripping people down to the bare bones of who they really were.

"You'll need to be checked out of the dorm by this weekend. Don't attend any more classes or soccer practices."

The pain on Jason's face brought tears to Adelaide's eyes.

She wanted to beg on his behalf. *Please don't do this to him. Please. There has to be another way. Why him and not Erin?* She glanced at Isaiah, but his expression remained unreadable. They'd discussed it, voted, and now Jason's future was destroyed by this high-and-mighty board.

"I don't understand." That was her voice, and her courage surprised her as much as everyone else. Isaiah nudged her knee with his own, but she ignored the hint. "Why can Erin stay and Jason can't?"

"I'm sorry, Mrs. English, but perhaps you don't understand the procedure taking place today."

"I fear I do. And it scares me. This isn't about rules, policies, or righting wrongs." Adelaide stood.

"Mrs. English!" James's voice rose. "Please be seated."

Isaiah tugged on her sleeve and whispered in a stern voice, "Adelaide, sit down."

She lowered herself to the edge of her chair. "I have to say this because if I don't, I'll regret it the rest of my life. You people are puppets. A powerful man decided the outcome of this meeting days ago, and you're allowing it! Erin warned me that her dad was after both Jason and me."

Rising again, she faced James. "Dr. Dunlap, you knew from the beginning that I wasn't right for this job, and you're correct. I can't work under such deceit and pretension. Though I'm certain you plan to fire me within minutes, there is no need. I resign. Now if you'll excuse me, I'll go pack up my room."

&

"Wow, didn't know she had it in her," Walt commented to Isaiah in a hushed tone as they left the meeting.

"She's right. James got the call. Chuck Martin told him how this would play out. They're even letting her walk at graduation! All he had to do was convince the board members to vote his way. In one day, three lives were drastically altered. Policy held fast for Jason and Addie, but not for Erin. Right now the whole system disgusts me."

"What is Adelaide going to do? According to Linda, the woman has no money."

"I figured as much. I don't know whether to admire her or think she's nuts. How many people with no means of support would quit their job on principle? I mean, she would have been fired, but she didn't know that for certain." He stopped in front of his outer office door. Rose smiled through the glass panes separating it from the hall. "Hey, I'll catch up with you later. I'm going to try to get Addie on her cell."

&.

After leaving the meeting, Adelaide returned to her apartment. Her legs felt like spaghetti. She fell across her bed, trying to catch her breath. What had she done? Was she nuts? "You have no job, Adelaide. What were you thinking?" She wasn't. Not at all.

She should pack, but she needed some fresh air. Grabbing her coat and cell phone, she headed out the door. For some reason, whenever she needed to clear her head, the river drew her. She opened her cell and pushed 3, walking toward the sound of the water.

"Hey, Addie. How are things going? You've been on my heart ever since I dropped you off at the airport yesterday."

"I quit my job."

"What?"

The one word echoed Adelaide's earlier question to herself. *Are you nuts?* "Sounds crazy, I know, but I did. They were seconds from firing me anyway."

Adelaide replayed the day for Monica—even her evolving feelings for Isaiah.

"Sounds like quite a day. What now?"

"I have no idea. I don't think I can stay here after the semester ends. I can't afford it." She made her way down the slope toward the river, finding the table—Isaiah's table—tucked in the trees.

"Come live with us and finish school here. I know Steve wouldn't mind."

"Thanks. I may have to take you up on that." She'd never felt so lost in her entire life. No money, and no place to go. Within weeks she could be homeless. That thought nearly paralyzed her. Of course Monica would never let that happen.

"Can I call you in a while? Isaiah's on the other line." But when she hung up, she decided not to switch over. She had to think. Her mind was reeling. Her stomach grew nauseous, and her head pounded. She sat on the cold cement bench, laid her head on the hard table, and cried. "God, are You there? My life just went from bad to worse."

Thank heaven she at least had the emergency fund she'd set aside. That would be enough to get her through this semester and home again. Home? She had no home. She had nothing except an expensive wardrobe she had no use for and a great collection of shoes and purses. "God, what do You want from me?"

eleven

Isaiah had been trying to call Addie for the past hour. Why wasn't she picking up? Was she okay? Had something happened? Finally he gave up his attempt to work. He'd go find her. He needed to see her and know she was all right.

He headed straight across the slushy earth where the grass had once been before the first snowfall. He made his way toward Zion Hall, pounding on her door several times.

Heather stuck her head out of her dorm room. "I don't think she's there."

"Sorry. You're right."

"If I see her, I'll let her know you're looking for her."

He nodded. "Have her call my cell."

He left the building, perched on a bench just outside, and hit REDIAL on his cell for the hundredth time. Still no answer. He left another message—just in case. Then he returned to her front door. This time, instead of knocking, he called her cell phone number again. He listened closely. No sound of ringing inside. Actually, no sounds at all. Either she was asleep with her ringer turned off, or she wasn't home. But where could she be? Glancing at his watch, he realized it would be dark in an hour.

He jogged around the building to the parking lot. Her car was there. That meant she was on foot. His gaze ran across the horizon. No sign of her anywhere. Maybe she went for a walk down by the river. Suddenly, in the frenzy of the search, he stopped. The truth hit him like a Mack truck. *I'm in love with her.* He felt just like he did when Julie slipped away from him and the cancer ravished her body. "I don't want to lose her, God. Don't let me lose her, too."

He took a deep breath and continued his trek toward the river, deciding to claim his favorite table and spend some time with the Lord instead of continuing the hunt for Addie. He needed to be recentered. As the table came into sight between the trees, he glimpsed Addie there—the woman who had no use for the great outdoors. The knowledge brought with it a tender smile. She'd remembered his favorite spot, and though she swore she wouldn't, she sought it out.

"Addie?"

She turned on the bench. Her tear-streaked face was beautiful to him. He rushed toward her, never taking his eyes from hers. She rose as he neared and stepped around the bench. He grabbed her and pulled her into his arms. She came willingly. He held her close to his heart, and she laid her head on his chest. He tangled his fingers in her hair. Neither said a word. But there were a million things he wanted to say. He had no idea how long they stood there; all he knew was that it felt right to hold her.

"It's almost dark," she whispered.

"I know." Neither made any effort to move.

"Maybe we should go."

"Maybe." But he didn't want to let go, not yet.

She raised her head. "What if someone sees us? I don't want to give the wrong impression. I know you're just a friend offering comfort, but to an onlooker it might not look so innocent."

He loosened his hold. "You're right, of course." She had no idea how he felt. It made him want to laugh. This was better anyway, with the proposal he had brewing in his head. He'd been wracking his brain for hours, trying to figure out a way she could stay in Idaho, stay in college, stay near him, and he had a plan.

She stepped out of his hold.

He let his empty arms drop to his sides. "Can I walk you back to the dorm?"

"I'd like that. Thank you." She smiled.

He shoved his hands in his pockets and raised his eyes to the rising moon.

"Isaiah, thank you."

"You're welcome, but you just thanked me ten seconds ago."

"Not for walking me back, but for the whole list of other things. You hired me when James didn't want to. You invested in me and encouraged me." She let out a long, slow sigh. "I'm sorry. I know my actions will cause you to reap repercussions. I didn't plan for it to end up like this."

"Me either."

She stopped. "Are you mad at me?"

"Of course not." He laughed. "I admire your guts today. The looks on their faces." He laughed harder.

She joined him. "I guess we both need some tension relief."

"Hey, why don't you shower and change, and I'll pick you up in an hour? We'll go to dinner—my treat—and you can fill me in on your next step."

"I'm not sure about the next step, but dinner sounds nice. Sitting home alone for the rest of the evening holds no appeal."

He stopped just outside the glass doors leading into Zion Hall. "See you soon. And dress warm. And kind of nice."

She nodded. "They were going to fire me, weren't they?"

He studied her for a moment. "What if I said no?" He smiled.

"Then I fear I might regret my words, but they were, right?"

He nodded. "They were."

"I feel so much better. I'd beat myself up for months if I'd thrown away everything on a wrong hunch."

"So you were intentional today?" He rubbed his chin.

"Sort of. Sort of spontaneous. But part of me figured if I was going to go out, I should go out in a blaze of glory."

He laughed again. "Well, blaze you did."

"Is there anything you can do for Jason?"

He shook his head. "Nope."

"What a waste of his talent, his brain, his ability. Can you at least help him get into another college that will let him pick up where he left off?"

"I'll look into it tomorrow. Here you are, more worried about him than yourself." His admiration for her grew almost daily as he saw another layer.

"He's young and has his whole life ahead. Can you fight for him to at least be able to take his exams so he doesn't lose the whole semester? Please fight for him."

"I'll see what I can do, but you have no requested favors for yourself, only for Jason? That's an admirable trait."

"Don't be impressed by me. If you only knew, I'm anything but admirable."

If you only knew, I admire just about everything I see, inside and out. "I'll remember that." He winked. "I'll remember, but I don't believe a word of it." He turned and left.

❧

Adelaide took extra effort getting ready. Every time she thought back to Isaiah holding her she smiled. He was who she'd miss the most. Not the college or the girls, but the man. Her schoolgirl crush—as she'd deemed it—seemed to be growing into a full-blown romance, but a one-sided romance. She'd be mortified if Isaiah had even an inkling of her growing feelings for him.

When she answered his knock an hour later, her heart responded to his smile. Her ruggedly handsome professor was dressed up tonight, well, at least for him. He'd ditched his jeans and Nikes for a pair of khaki Dockers, a sweater, and penny loafers.

"You clean up nice." She retreated into her living room to grab her purse and coat.

"So do you. Hey, you've already started packing." His gaze roamed over the few boxes stacked in the corner.

"Yep. I'd like to be out in the next couple of days." She pulled her door shut and locked the dead bolt.

He held the glass door open. The cool night air blew through. "What then?"

"I'm not sure." She hunkered deeper into her coat.

"There's only a couple of weeks left in the semester. At least finish." He held his car door open for her.

"I probably will." She buckled her seat belt. "Linda offered me a guest room for the next few weeks."

"You know, you could still stick around and finish your degree." He started the car.

"I thought about that, but I need a job. I guess that should be my starting point and the determining factor. I can't stay without a means to support myself."

"What kind of job would you like?" He turned down a road she wasn't familiar with—the opposite direction of town.

She half-snorted, half-laughed. "Like? How about a CEO of a major corporation? What am I qualified for? A fast-food joint."

He parked the car in front of the Cedars. "Coeur d'Alene's

finest dining. It's a floating restaurant directly across the river from the campus."

"I think I've seen it when I've walked down by the river, but didn't know what it was."

He helped her from the car.

"Such a gentleman. Thank you."

He smiled and in the moonlit night was even more appealing. Tucking her arm through his, he led her down the plank to the front door. He spoke to the hostess while she took in her elegant surroundings. This was the type of place she and Harold had frequented in Dallas.

She followed the hostess, and Isaiah followed her with his hand on the small of her back. If he only knew how his touch affected her. For him it was a polite gesture, but for her it sent shivers up her spine. When they arrived at their table, he helped her out of her coat and pulled out her chair. The hostess took their coats, and they settled in with their menus.

Adelaide soon laid hers down and studied the man across from her. He was busy with his menu, so she had complete freedom to gawk. She admired his strong jaw, the lines time had carved into his face, and his gentle eyes. When he looked up, she averted her gaze, embarrassed.

"What are you thinking?"

Panic washed over her. *I'm thinking about you.* Did he somehow know that?

He glanced back at the menu. "I'm thinking salmon."

She smiled in relief. "Me, too."

He laid his menu down. "So you've seen this place from the river?"

She nodded, gazing out the window. The lights on the water were beautiful.

"I thought you didn't like the outdoors much." His grin mocked her.

"I'm learning. It's so pretty here, and there is something so peaceful about being outside, especially listening to the river race by." She felt silly that it had taken her this many years to figure out how to enjoy God's gifts to her.

"I know what you mean." His face reflected an inner contentment that she still only hoped for.

The waiter brought their iced teas. Isaiah stirred some sugar into his. "When we were talking about jobs earlier, I heard about one that might interest you."

"Really?" She sat up straighter, leaning forward.

"I don't want you to be offended." Concern painted his face.

She laughed. "What kind of job is this? Surely not something immoral."

Now he laughed. "Of course not!" He hesitated. "A housekeeper." He studied her with great intensity.

She thought about it a moment. Then the irony hit her. "I used to have one, now I am one?"

"Bad idea?"

She sat back in her chair. "I don't know. I never thought about that sort of job before."

"Here's the thing, the job comes with a place to live, allowing you to finish your college education."

"Is it for some hoity-toity family?" The way some of Harold's friends treated their maids was atrocious.

"Not necessarily. I mean, there are many jobs of that type, but the one I'm speaking of is a rather down-to-earth family." He buttered a roll. "You came here with this dream that you'd carried in your heart all those years. Dreams are worth fighting for. One door closes, you prayerfully find another door."

"Or maybe you just realize the dream is no longer attainable." At least that's what she felt at this moment.

The salads arrived, and Isaiah blessed their meal.

"In order to finish school, you need a job that provides housing and some cash, right?"

She nodded, chewing.

"So as far as I can figure, there are several jobs in that category besides working at the college. A caretaker for the elderly, a nanny, or a live-in housekeeper. My guess is the last one will give you the most time for school and studying."

This time she scrutinized him. "You've given this a lot of thought."

"I have."

"Why?"

He broke eye contact, focusing on his salad.

"I don't want you to leave. . .school."

His words increased her heart rate. *I don't want you to leave.* Nor did she want to leave, but then he added that one extra word, changing the entire meaning and connotation.

"So I spent all day searching for a solution, and this job came to mind. Could be your answer."

"Why does it matter to you if I leave school? I don't understand why you'd care."

"I hate to see anyone leave school, ever, until they're done. Education is hard, it's expensive, and it has to be a priority or it will fall through the cracks." He'd shifted into his professor mode. "If you don't finish, what will you do to support yourself for the rest of your life? Do you really want to work in some menial job? You're young, Addie. You have a lot of years ahead of you. Don't you want the opportunity to do something that you love versus taking whatever job you can find to pay the bills?"

She'd originally thought he might have some personal reason for wanting her to stay, but he quickly burst that bubble of hope with his education speech. "You're right. I wasn't thinking long-term. Tell me more about the job."

"Cooking and laundry in exchange for a small salary and your own private guest cottage."

She remembered his place had a guest cottage. "Is this for you?"

He nodded.

"The A-frame next to your house?"

"Yep."

"Isaiah, I don't want a pity job."

Their salmon arrived, and the waiter cleared their salad plates.

"What, may I ask, is a pity job?" His eyes bored into her.

"It's you giving me a job because you feel sorry for me." She sliced off a bite of salmon with her fork.

"It's not like that, honest. I had another lady until a couple of months ago. Her husband was transferred out of state. I thought I'd give it a shot myself, but it isn't working for me. I just don't have time with the horses and school. The place is a mess. Believe me, you'll earn your pay."

The horses. As she'd grown more enamored with the man, she'd let that issue slip her mind. Could she bring herself to live on a ranch that raised racehorses and ultimately contributed to gambling?

"It would solve a problem for both of us. You could stay in college, and I could quit digging through the laundry hamper to find something to wear."

Giggling, she said, "You don't really, do you?"

"I've thought about it once or twice."

Maybe she'd made too big a deal over the horse issue. She

chewed another bite of her dinner. No one, not even Monica, agreed with her. And all their examples did shoot holes in her theories. Monica had said that the truth was, morality could not be legislated. People would gamble whether Isaiah raised horses or not. Adelaide sipped her tea. *Monica's right, and Isaiah is a good man.* She needed to let go of the horse issue. This opportunity would allow her to finish school and make a way for herself in the world. She didn't like this hand-to-mouth living. And if she left school, she'd have to take charity from her friend to survive. She set her tea glass down.

"I'll take the job." Did she really have a choice?

"What? You will?"

She grinned at him. "My answer obviously surprised you."

"In a good way." He raised his water glass. "To my new cleaning lady."

She clanked her glass against his.

"Did you really used to have your own maid and cook?" he asked.

She'd not shared her past with anyone in Idaho. Was she ready? *Be real, be honest, be yourself.* Lissa's words haunted her at the most inopportune times.

"And a gardener and pool man."

Isaiah laid down his fork. "You're kidding."

She shook her head.

"I'll buy you dessert and coffee if you'll tell me your story." He slid his empty plate toward the middle of the table.

Adelaide ran fingertips over the pearls draped around her neck. "I don't know if you'll find it worth much, but you've got a deal."

twelve

Adelaide ordered crème brûlée and coffee. He followed her lead.

"Just a warning, this story could get emotional."

He raised his cloth napkin off his lap. "I have just the tools to handle tears."

The waiter brought their coffee cups. She took her time adding cream and sugar, stirring until it was just right. She laid her spoon across the saucer. "My father was military."

He hadn't expected her to go back that far.

"Authoritarian. Lots of rules, not much for relationship. A lot of kids have it worse, and I know that, but my growing-up years were sometimes difficult."

An extra sheen of moisture heightened the color of her brown eyes.

"*Strict, harsh,* and *critical* are words I'd use to describe my father. All law, no grace."

"Ah, thus your concern to extend grace to Jason and Erin."

"Yes. Second chances are big in my book." Dabbing her mouth with her napkin, she continued, "My teen years were hard. We butted heads a lot, and I always lost because it was his way or the highway. My senior year I met Harold. He was my best friend's cousin and way too old for me at twenty-five, but I caught his eye, nonetheless. And I was just what he was looking for." Bitterness had crept into her tone.

The waiter delivered their desserts. Addie took the opportunity to compose herself. She spooned out her first bite. "This is heaven."

Isaiah tasted his. "I've got to agree."

"Thank you for tonight. The food's been great, and this place is lovely."

"And the company?" He joked to lighten the mood and wondered if she'd gone as far into her past as she could tonight. It had been an emotional day all the way around.

"The company—well, let's see," she drawled. "Passable."

"Passable? To an educator like me, *passable* is no compliment."

"Seriously, you're easy to be with and a great listener. If not for you and Linda, I'd have no friends here at all."

He adopted his best hurt expression. "Passable, easy to be with, great listener. Sounds like the description of a golden retriever. I'm going to have to work on my people skills."

She reached across the table and patted his hand. "Poor Dr. Shepherd. You want complete honesty?"

He raised his brows. "I don't know. How much worse can this get?"

She laughed, and he joined her. "I enjoy your company very much and value your friendship. And interestingly enough, you're my first and only male friend since high school."

"Really?"

"Really. And based on the men in my past—my father and Harold—easy to be with is a high compliment."

So, she'd had a tough marriage. He'd suspected as much.

She sipped her coffee. "On with the story, or have I bored you to tears?"

"Nope, but are you up for finishing it?"

She pondered his question. "I don't know, but I feel it needs to be told."

"Sometimes the past loses its power when we share it. What

did you mean when you said you were just what Harold was looking for?"

"He thought I was beautiful and would make an ideal trophy wife. Eye candy to hang on his arm."

"You are beautiful, but that and so much more. You're bright, hardworking—"

"Please." She waved off his praise. "Anyway, I wanted a way out of my father's control, and Harold wanted me. Mutual need is a beautiful thing until you try to build a marriage on it."

"So you married the guy?"

"I barely knew him. Said 'I do' the day after high school graduation and three months after meeting him. Moved to Texas the day after a modest wedding in the chapel at Tinker Air Force Base in Oklahoma City. I started college once we settled in, but my schedule didn't mesh well with Harold's, so after a couple of years, I gave up."

He waited while she took another bite of dessert and a few sips of coffee. His heart ached for what she'd missed. He and Julie shared a beautiful relationship. It sounded like she hadn't experienced anything like that.

"Harold made a lot of money, and we lived the good life. Upper-crust Dallas social scene—parties, benefits, culture. But in many ways, he was just like my father. He ran the ship; my opinion mattered little. He did what he wanted, when he wanted, and I did what he wanted, when he wanted, and had better look good doing it."

"I'm sorry."

"I sold myself into slavery. Traded one set of miserable circumstances for another. But the great thing is, I got my daughter out of the deal, and she's wonderful and makes it all worth it."

"You said your daughter is at Wheaton? Was your husband a Christian?"

"Yes, she's finishing her senior year, and he claimed to be a Christian. Only God knows."

"If you don't mind my asking, what happened to the money?"

"Gambling."

The aversion to his horses—it all made sense now. "Did he lose everything?"

"If he hadn't conveniently died when he did, he probably would have, but instead he had a massive heart attack and left the mess for Lissa and I to deal with. Just days after his passing bill collectors were calling, a loan shark knocking at the front door. My suburban life turned into a nightmare."

"Did you try to get him help?"

"I didn't know. Sometimes I suspected something wasn't right, but I didn't have the courage to confront. I tried to live by the old adage that what you don't know can't hurt you. As you know, that one is a lie. And as you probably figured out by now, it's also my biggest downfall." Tears pooled in her large brown eyes.

"Maybe if I'd confronted him, he'd have gotten help and stopped. Maybe if I'd been forthright about Erin and Jason, things would have turned out differently. At least I wouldn't have lost my job. The thing about strongholds is they never just go away, and each time they rear their ugly heads, the problem is worse and the hold tighter." She suddenly looked embarrassed. "I'm sorry. I didn't mean to spill my whole life all over you."

"No problem. Someday I'll spill mine all over you." He glanced at his watch. "I guess I'd better get you back. It's been a long day."

"Too long," she agreed.

❧

Adelaide had two messages from Monica and one from Lissa. She called Lissa first because of the time difference. Lissa was already in bed, so Adelaide gave her a quick overview of the day from the pit. Then she called Monica, who was a night owl by nature and still awake.

"I was worried when you didn't call back. Glad life's under control."

Adelaide assured her that she was fine and would survive this unexpected turn of events. Then she told her about Isaiah's job offer. "Did I make a mistake?"

Monica was quiet a minute. "Completely separate residence?"

"Yes."

"No secret staircase?"

Laughing, she said, "Not unless it's buried underground. The houses are separated by a chunk of land. I'm not good at guessing how many feet, but you could park several cars between them." She paused, but Monica said nothing. "You do think I made a mistake, don't you? I can still tell him thanks but no thanks."

"It sounds like a respectable arrangement, but honestly, I'd feel better if his sons were around."

"Surely you don't think we're going to mess around?" The idea amused Adelaide.

"You are both healthy, physically attractive adults, alone out in the country. It might be a risky setup."

"First of all, we have no evidence that he is in any way attracted to me."

"Oh, come on. Is there a man alive who doesn't consider you beautiful?"

"That doesn't necessarily mean they are attracted to me. But even if all you said were true, he's a godly man, a man of integrity. He would never let something like that happen between us."

"He's a man. You're a woman. Neither of you have had sex in a very long time. David was a man after God's heart, and it happened to him. Don't tell me it can't happen."

"You're right. We are all susceptible to temptation. It is hard, however, for me to imagine ever wanting a man in that way again. I didn't even want Harold, and he was right next to me in bed."

"That was different. He tried to love you with money, and it didn't meet your emotional needs. It's hard to make love to a man who only wants you for sex and to parade you around as a personal trinket. You're already crushing on Isaiah. I'd guess the outcome with him will be quite different."

She had to admit that on more than one occasion she'd wished for his kiss. It had been years since she'd longed for a kiss from Harold.

"Okay, I'm convinced. There is risk. You've always been my spiritual mentor, so I'm asking, what should I do?"

"Set good boundaries."

"Like what?"

"You don't clean when he's home or even go in his house when he's there. He doesn't come into your place either. You can share a cup of coffee on the porch, but avoid any togetherness at his place. If he wants to spend time with you, he can invite you out on a date."

"Wow, you're tough." Adelaide felt like she'd been sent back to the air force base to live with her dad.

"You've got to be when taking on a very real enemy who'd love to ruin both your reputations. He especially loves to go after people whom others respect, like Isaiah. The higher you are, the farther you fall."

"So I need to set these boundaries verbally with Isaiah?"

"Yep. Otherwise how will he know? Why don't you take the job on a temporary basis and do a thorough search during Christmas break? If God opens another door, good. If not, stay. Finding another job that will fit your school schedule and provide enough money to live on and pay for college will be nearly impossible, so if it happens, you'll know it's God."

"Okay." Made sense to her.

"Are you sure you want to stay there? Why don't you come back to Dallas, live with us, and make your fresh start here?"

"It's hard to make a fresh start in an old environment. It's been nice to be so far away from Harold's friends and their pity."

"If that's what you want. I just always want you to know you've got a place to stay here with us."

"You guys are great friends, and I won't forget your offer. If I ever do need a place, you'll be the first to know." Adelaide loaded her bathroom cleaning supplies into a cardboard box while they chatted.

"I only wish we were going to be home for Christmas so you and Lissa could spend the holiday with us."

"Christmas in Germany with Jen will be a pretty tough sacrifice."

Monica's laughter carried over the line. "I cannot wait. Did I tell you Jen, Roger, and the kids along with Steve and me are going to Tuscany for a week?"

"You did. Sounds wonderful. As you know, Harold was never one to travel much for personal pleasure. Said his consulting company took him too far too often. Had no desire to travel for fun and leisure. Besides, he was too busy making and spending money." She sealed the box shut with packing tape. "When do you leave?"

"Next week. We're gone almost a month. I'll miss talking to you, but won't stop praying. Just promise me that if you move in and things start to get intimate, you'll tell me. I can offer accountability."

"Yeah, and you see how well that went with Jason and Erin." She stacked the box onto the growing heap in her living room. Now she was glad she'd flattened and saved these moving boxes under her bed.

"She may have already been pregnant. You don't know for sure that they didn't stop once they met with you."

"No, but if I had to guess, I think I got lip service. You know the saddest part to me? I feel like she sold Jason out to save her own hide. I was watching her this morning and am sure she knew how all this would play out. There was no surprise, nor sorrow for that matter, when the board announced Jason's expulsion. How can she claim to love the guy, yet let her father destroy his future?" She unloaded her nightstand into another box.

"He's the real reason that I resigned. I couldn't work here if they allow parents to buy favors because of the size of their donations. I don't know how Isaiah does it."

"That's politics. It's everywhere now, even in Christian organizations."

"What's Jason going to do? He'll most likely lose this semester. My heart breaks for him the most. And will he ever even get to see his own child? Life isn't fair, is it? I tell you, if I had Harold's money, I'd make a difference for kids like him."

"You're passionate about this."

"I am."

"You're different, Addie. And I like this new you. You're less fearful and more likely to speak your mind."

She stopped packing and looked into the mirror above her

dresser. "I am, and I think I like it." She smiled, noting the long-missing spark had returned to her eyes. "And it's thanks to God, Isaiah, and my daughter. I think I told you that I've been memorizing verses on fear and asking God for the kind of freedom I see in Isaiah. And Lissa nags me all the time to reinvent myself into the person God intended instead of the woman Harold demanded."

"Well, I like the new Adelaide English. You're bolder, braver, and more confident."

"I guess it's easier to have more confidence when you don't constantly have someone criticizing you and trying to remake you into the image of his perfect woman."

"I would think so. You know what's always surprised me? He put so much pressure on you, yet he was able to accept and love Lissa without the demands."

"That was God, and I'm so grateful. I prayed from her conception that he wouldn't be the kind of dad mine was. By then, circumstances indicated that he had that leaning. He was a much better dad than a husband."

"You are right about that. Hey, it's almost two here. Guess I should hit the sack. Love you, friend."

❧

Isaiah fired up his truck early the next morning. He decided he'd help Addie move before she had a chance to change her mind. Moving her over would take no time at all. Good thing the cottage was fully supplied because other than fashion-related items, the woman traveled light. Wow, she'd had quite the life, rich but relationally poor. And now she had nothing. The stress of all Harold's gambling debt probably killed him.

Isaiah knocked on Adelaide's door at seven sharp. He only rapped lightly, so as not to disturb the entire middle section of Zion Hall. He thought he caught the sound of some rustling inside. Sure enough, the chain on the inside of the door was being released. She peeped out.

"Isaiah! What time is it?"

"It's seven. I came to help you move." He kept his voice low.

"Are you nuts? Seven a.m.?" Her eyes squinted against the offending light.

"I've been up a couple of hours and am raring to go."

"I've been asleep a couple of hours. Can you come back later?" She started to shut the door, but he reached out and caught it before it clicked shut.

"I only have until nine. The rest of my day is full."

She shook her head. "How do you know I didn't change my mind?"

"Just a hunch. Tell you what, you set all your boxes outside the door, and I'll load and haul them back to the cottage. You can head up there later today or whenever you're ready to unpack."

"Will that make you disappear?"

He laughed, and she handed him a load of boxes stacked four high. While he carried those out to the truck, she stacked the rest just outside the door. By the time he returned, she was stacking the last couple.

"That it?"

"Yes." She stepped back into her apartment.

"What time will you be done with class today?"

"Four."

"Perfect. I'll meet you out at my place about fifteen minutes later. Show you around, help you unpack."

Adelaide bit her bottom lip. "About that. Maybe not such a good idea. I've been told I need to set boundaries to protect us both."

He laughed. "Walt told me the same thing."

"Front porches only?" She yawned.

"Yep, pretty much."

"Okay. Your porch or mine?"

"Yours." It would be as natural as breathing to place his index finger under her chin and bend to meet her lips. Yep—as natural as breathing. Instead he took a step backward. "See you soon."

He grabbed several boxes and headed toward the truck. Walt was right. He'd have to set firm lines and not cross them. Having her around could be more tempting than he'd originally thought. He'd adhere to the same rules the college enforced—no dating the hired help. Walt offered to take her off his hands if things got too sticky. Always good to have a plan B.

❧

"This is Scooter. I'm going to breed her one more time in the spring, and then she'll get to retire."

Adelaide stroked her velvet nose. "Hey, pretty girl."

"You still remember how to saddle a horse?" Isaiah asked.

"I think I could figure it out."

"Then she's yours anytime you feel like riding."

"Mine? Anytime I want to ride." What a dream come true. "Thank you! Would you ride with me sometime?"

"How about Saturday?"

"You have yourself a date." *A date! What am I saying?* She felt her cheeks growing warmer. "I mean, not a date, but a deal."

His grin widened. "Of course not a date. I never took it that way."

She decided a diversion was needed. "Where do you usually ride?"

"Did you see those mountains up behind my house? Well,

there are some great trails up there with killer views. Maybe we'll take a picnic lunch and make a date—uh, day—a day of it."

She liked this playful, joking side of him, but it only increased his appeal. Why did he have to be so cute, anyway? "I will put you and Scooter on my calendar. Maybe you can saddle her the first time, rather than trusting my memory."

She helped him feed the animals and enjoyed learning their names and some of their history. "What do you do with a horse once you retire them?"

"I often look for a kid who's searching for a starter horse. They give them a good home, and by the time the horse passes, the kid is ready to move on to bigger and better things."

"So someday might I inherit Scooter?"

He eyed her, wearing a serious expression. "I said a kid, and in my book, you are a long way from that."

"Hey! Never kid a woman about her age."

"Well then, you just might."

I think I'd rather inherit you. That wayward thought surprised her.

thirteen

Adelaide started brown-bagging her lunches since she no longer lived on campus. As soon as her Lit class was dismissed, she threw her backpack over her shoulder and headed out the door toward her favorite table in the cafeteria—the table for two, back in the corner, next to the window. She pulled out her lunch and spread it before her. Today was yogurt, a banana, and a small salad. Then she pulled out her Bible to work on some OT homework. It was still her favorite class. She kept telling herself it had nothing to do with her prof—but who was she kidding?

Strange, she'd lived at Isaiah's place for ten days now and rarely saw him. She'd seen him much more often when she lived and worked on campus. They had ridden together last Saturday. Boy, was it good to straddle a horse again. They'd not talked a lot, but just enjoyed the outdoors. Idaho was beautiful, much different from what she'd expected. Potatoes were what came to mind before living here. Now it was rugged wilderness filled with rivers, mountains, and breathtaking scenery.

"Mrs. E., do you have a minute?" Heather pulled her out of contemplation and back to the present.

"Sure. Have a seat." Adelaide shifted her things to her side of the table. "Do you want to join me for lunch?"

"No thanks. I just wanted to make sure you're okay."

Her care touched Adelaide's heart. She was the only student who'd even approached her since her firing. "I'm doing all right. Trying to figure out whether to stick this out for the next three and a half years or tuck tail and run."

"I'm sorry you were let go."

"Me, too." Adelaide's words tripped over the lump lodged in her throat, making them raspy. "Me, too. One reason running sounds pretty appealing." She forced a smile to lighten the mood. "As my mom used to say, such is life."

Heather studied her intently. "There's a lot of gossip going around."

"I'm not surprised." She wanted to inquire as to who was saying what, but figured in the long run, she'd be better off not knowing.

"A lot of people seem to think you're living with Dr. Shepherd."

Adelaide gasped. "What?"

"I didn't believe it," Heather assured her. "But I thought you should know."

So much for being better off not knowing. "I took a job as his housekeeper and live in a small cottage on his property, but we do not live together. I haven't even seen the man in days."

"So you're not dating?"

"No." Adelaide shook her head. "Where do all these rumors come from?"

Heather shrugged. "A lot of us saw him moving you out of the dorm, and somebody followed him to see where he was taking your stuff. When he took it to his place. . ."

Adelaide's chest tightened, and breathing became more difficult. "This is crazy. Why don't people check their facts?"

"Well, not only did he haul your stuff to his house, rumor has it you two were seen at the Cedars looking quite cozy." Heather's expression was apologetic.

"You've got to be kidding me. Don't these people have

better things to do than report my every move?" Adelaide's heart rate increased.

"I thought I should tell you."

Part of her was thankful, but another part wished to roll back the clock ten minutes.

"Anything else?"

"The complete story is pretty bad, Mrs. E. I don't know if you really want to know."

Oh, now she decides to use discretion? "Look, Heather, since you've already spilled half the beans, you might as well empty the whole can." She hoped she'd not regret that choice.

Heather glanced away. "I may have already said too much." She squirmed in her seat.

"You may have, but now I want to know."

"You and Dr. Shepherd are living together, sleeping together, and you're the biggest hypocrite on the planet."

The words stung and knocked the wind from her lungs.

"Heather, none of that is true. I explained why I live on his property. He offered me a job, and since I lost the one here, I desperately needed one."

The girl nodded. "I'm here because I believe you."

"Why do people think I'm a hypocrite?"

"Because you tried to get Erin and Jason kicked out of school for their indiscretion when you and our prof are doing the same thing."

Adelaide blinked, fighting off the threatening tears. "Heather, none of that is true. Dr. Shepherd and I are barely friends. He took me to dinner the night I was fired because I think he just plain felt sorry for me. I have no friends or family within a few thousand miles." She realized her voice had risen as she made her passionate plea. Glancing up, the people at several nearby tables gawked.

She lowered her tone to a whisper. "I fought for Jason and Erin. That's why I lost my job—because I *didn't* report them, not because I did." Picking up her napkin, Adelaide dabbed her eyes, hoping to catch the moisture before it wreaked havoc with her makeup.

"You fought for them? That's not what Erin said." Heather followed Adelaide's lead and spoke in a whisper.

The girl might as well have stuck a knife in Adelaide's heart. "Erin said that? You heard her yourself?"

Heather nodded.

"Please tell me exactly what she said." Adelaide leaned in, wanting to catch not just the words but the way they were said.

" 'Mrs. E. was fired because she turned on Jason and me. She went to the board to get us expelled, but the surprise was on her because my dad fought back. Poor Jason was the scapegoat, thanks to her. If she hadn't made a big deal out of our mistake, he'd still be in school.' "

"Why? Why would she lie? I don't understand." She searched Heather's face. "You have to believe me. None of that ever happened. Will you tell people the truth, please?"

Heather shrugged. "I can try, but I don't know what good it will do."

Now the tears flowed freely over Adelaide's cheeks. Her heart ached with the ramifications of all the gossip, slander, and lies. Her head hung in embarrassment and shame. No one really knew her, and now she'd been branded as a bad seed, a troublemaker, and how could she prove otherwise?

"Mrs. E.?" Heather laid her hand on Adelaide's arm. "Are you okay?"

"No. No, Heather, I'm not. Lies hurt innocent people."

"Adelaide?"

She raised her tear-soaked face. Linda stood over her, concern creasing her brows.

"I'll let you talk to her." Heather nearly jumped from the chair, offering it to Linda.

Adelaide had probably traumatized the poor girl with her over-the-top emotions. "I'm sorry I fell apart. I appreciate your honesty." Did she? Not so much at the moment.

"And I'm sorry. Mrs. E., I didn't mean to hurt you. I just know if it were me, I'd want to know." With those words, Heather scampered away as quickly as she'd come.

Linda pulled some tissues from her purse. "What in the world did she say to you?"

Adelaide dried her cheeks with the fresh white Kleenex. "It wasn't her. She was just the messenger." She went on to fill Linda in on the fifteen-minute conversation she and Heather just shared.

"Oh, Adelaide, I'm so sorry." Compassion laced each word.

Adelaide appreciated her sincerity. "What now?"

Linda shook her head. "Gossip and slander are hard to beat off, even with the truth. I think that's why God warns us not to partake in either, but for some people it's their sin of choice. I guess we all have something."

First Harold's sin had devastated their whole family and lives, and now some student's lies were destroying her reputation. *God, what am I supposed to do? Why are You letting this happen?* Then she remembered what had happened to her friend Janice at the hospital where she worked prior to Lissa's birth.

"At my old job, one of my coworkers decided she didn't like a new girl we'd hired. We were all three equals, but Debbie wanted to treat Janice as if she were inferior, even though Janice had more experience and expertise in the field. Debbie wanted to run the show and have Janice do the grunt work. Finally, after months of enduring Debbie's criticisms and constant control, Janice stood up for herself, but first she went to her boss to make sure she understood what she was actually hired to do. Was she Debbie's assistant, or was she hired to do an equal portion of the job with equal responsibility?

"Once that was clear, she went to counseling because she wasn't sure how to handle the situation and honor God at the same time. Following the counselor's instructions, she quietly called Debbie out for overstepping the boundaries. Made Debbie mad. No one had ever called her on her stuff before. She stormed out of the office, telling everyone who'd listen her version of the story. Poor Janice didn't know what hit her. People started treating her differently. Most, of course, believed Debbie because she'd been there many years." As Adelaide remembered the destruction the slander caused, she felt more hopeless all the time.

"Are you trying to cheer yourself up? Because I don't think it's working."

"I guess I just want you to realize what I'm up against." Adelaide sniffed. "I know. I walked through it with a friend. Debbie's version of the story damaged Janice on every level, but she was determined to get through it and honor God. I became her confidant, and my heart ached for her. She refused to gossip back and didn't even defend herself, though she wanted to in every way. She fought the urge to go to each person and proclaim her innocence. The hard part was watching other people treat her differently based on a lie. She just kept asking God to fight her battle and expose the truth of the situation."

"Again, I'm so sorry. But the employees of the college won't believe Erin's story, only the students." Linda patted her hand.

"But I am a student. Don't you get it? I'm one of them, and I already stick out like a sore thumb. This will only serve to make it that much harder. I don't think I can do it." Adelaide shut her Bible and started shoving her things into her book bag.

"What are you saying?"

"Have you heard of the straw that broke the camel's back?"

"Certainly." Linda nodded.

"This was my straw. I can't do this anymore." Adelaide rose, pulling her book bag over her right shoulder. "I'm going home—back to Dallas. I hate this college."

Linda grabbed her arm. "Wait. At least finish the semester so you don't lose everything. You only have a week left after this one and then finals week. Move in with us, but stick it out. You'll regret it if you don't."

"I don't know if I can." Adelaide glanced around the cafeteria. It felt as though many people were glancing her direction and whispering. Was she being paranoid? "I just want to go home." She rudely left Linda standing there, but her need to escape was stronger than her desire for polite propriety.

Home. If only there was one somewhere to run to.

❧

Isaiah rubbed the back of his neck. This had been the toughest semester he could remember—ever. With the Erin and Jason ordeal, Addie losing her job, and James breathing down his neck like never before. The grapevine carried rumors of the college president retiring at year's end. Isaiah believed James was politicking for the position and wanted to discredit Isaiah and Walt as much as possible in case they were contenders. What was wrong with letting God direct instead of mudslinging? Were those days gone even in Christian arenas?

A knock on his open door brought his gaze up from the computer screen to James. Great. What did he want now?

"You have a minute?"

"Sure."

James closed the door, and Isaiah knew another serious matter had arisen. James settled into a chair across the desk from Isaiah, his face draped in concern.

Isaiah shot up a quick prayer for patience. He was in no mood for more drama today, or James's antics for that matter.

James cleared his throat and met Isaiah's gaze with a challenge in his own. "I understand you've moved Adelaide English out to your place."

Isaiah bristled, not liking the inference. "Yes, she's living in the cottage next door and has taken the job as my cleaning lady."

"Cleaning lady? Convenient."

"Look, James, get to the point. I've got a lot to do and don't appreciate your insinuations."

James leaned forward in his chair. "I have reports that not only are the two of you living together—"

"Living together? Living together?!" Isaiah stood, towering above his desk and James. "How dare you! Not only do you defame me, but Mrs. English as well. Do you think I would do that? Have you no respect for me as a Christian? I've never even held the woman's hand, and no, we are not living together. I have a neighbor on the other side of me who is a widow as well. Am I living with her, too?" He was hot, and that didn't happen often.

"I'm sorry if I've offended you, but these reports are flying around the college."

"They're not reports, James. They are gossip. Now if you've got nothing more to do with your time than listen to slanderous innuendo, maybe you need to rethink your job description because as my boss, you should be offended for me, not concerned about the validity of the reports. Now, if you'll excuse me."

Isaiah walked out, leaving James sitting there. He needed to clear his head with a good run, but a higher priority was to find Addie before she caught wind of this. The news could devastate her. He'd worked here long enough to know rumors came and went, most forgotten within weeks.

Using his key, he ducked into Walt's office. Linda wasn't in the outer office, nor was Walt in his. Isaiah would borrow Walt's computer to track Adelaide's whereabouts. He pushed Walt's door almost shut in case James wandered by. Pretty sure Adelaide had a class right about now, he signed on, went to the schedule module, and found she had a Christian Thought class in the D Pod. As he was signing off, Walt and Linda arrived.

After an explanation of what he was doing, Linda updated him on the fact that Adelaide had already heard the gossip. Linda filled him in on Adelaide's frame of mind.

"I was afraid that would happen." He tilted his head back and let out a sigh. "Any idea where she went?"

"None. I tried to stall her, but she took off. Honestly, Zay, I wouldn't be at all surprised if she was on the next plane to Dallas."

His heart fell to his knees. *Don't leave, Addie, not yet. Give me a chance to win your love.* "I hope not."

"Do you want us to help you look?" Walt offered.

"No." He wanted to be the one to find her. "At least not yet, but thanks. You can, however, pray."

As he headed out the office door, Linda called after him. "Let us know when you find her."

He jogged over to the D Pod, trying to be inconspicuous as he waited for her class to dismiss. For some reason he doubted she was there, but he'd check anyway.

He'd kept his distance since she'd moved into the A-frame, realizing God had some healing to do before she'd be ready to love again. Harold had broken not only her heart, but her trust as well. She'd need to forgive him before she could trust another man. He'd hoped another semester and a new job and place of residence would put her in a good place for them to start dating. Now it looked as though they'd never get that chance.

The door flew open, and students poured out. His eyes never left the flow of people coming out of the classroom. He waited and watched, but no Addie. He hoped no one noticed him hovering. It might only add to the rumor mill if someone saw him and did the deductive reasoning.

Now where? The river? The A-frame? The airport? Addie was a creature of habit, so he'd check out "her" parking lot first. That would help him decide whether the search should begin on campus or off. Seemed he'd done this just a couple of weeks ago. *Adelaide English, you are under my skin and in my heart. . . .*

He fought the urge to jog or run, trying to appear as nonchalant as possible. He wondered what Erin's game was. Addie took a risk and lost for her and Jason. What did she hope to gain by hurting her? If anything, the girl should be groveling at Adelaide's feet, asking her for forgiveness, not spreading lies.

He rounded the corner of Zion Hall and had a clear view of the parking lot. His gaze shot from one end to the other. No sign of Addie or her SUV. He closed his eyes. *God, don't let her be on the way to the airport.* He felt inches away from losing her, and she wasn't even his to lose.

fourteen

Adelaide had followed the river all the way down to the resort. First she cried, then she talked to God, and now she sat on a curb and pushed the number 3 on her cell phone. "I'm so glad it's today and not tomorrow, because tomorrow Monica would be on her way to Germany," she whispered as the phone rang. Adelaide so needed to hear the voice of someone who loved her.

"Hello?"

She burst into tears, recounting her whole lunchtime ordeal.

"I can call and get you a ticket right now, if that's what you want, but maybe running isn't the answer."

"Is that what I'd be doing? Running?"

"Sort of." Monica's tone was gentle to soften her honesty.

"Did I run here, too?" She did. Suddenly the truth was crystal clear, as if the Lord removed a veil. "I did." She answered her own question before Monica had the chance.

"I don't think following your dream was wrong," Monica reassured her. "But maybe you should have let God heal your heart before you left."

The words rang true. She'd left before she'd forgiven. She'd tried to run and hide from what Harold did to her and Lissa, but there was no hiding. The hurt, disappointment, and bitterness moved with her to Idaho. Now more had been added to the growing list of unfairness in her life.

"Can I share some things with you that Mike Bickle

preached on this past Sunday that might help?"

"Sure." Adelaide smiled. Her friend never failed to point her back to Christ.

"I think it applies to both Erin and Harold, but you see what you think. Can we pray first?"

At Adelaide's agreement, Monica prayed for the truth to set Addie free. *Free.* Just the word brought an ache to her heart. Had she ever been truly free? Surely not in years, if ever. She'd been weighed down by fear, unforgiveness, and bitterness. Not just since Harold's death, but the negative emotions toward him had been piling up for years, nearly a lifetime. And suddenly Adelaide knew—God was ready to do business. Anticipation mounted on wings like eagles. Right here, right now, she and God were settling past debts. Heart pounding, she swallowed.

Monica finished with an "amen."

"I'm ready." And she was.

"Let me grab my notes. They are right here. Okay. Maintaining order in conflict starts with giving blessing."

"What does that mean? How do I do it?"

"Well, with Harold, you can't, but with Erin you treat her in ways that will bless her—kindness, smiles, words well spoken. And in a way, I guess you can with Harold, too. Thank God for those twenty-plus years of marriage and for the man he was. Maybe even thank Him for the man he wasn't. After all, it was some of his imperfections that drove you to the Lord." Every word Monica spoke rang true and resounded in Adelaide's spirit.

"All right, start with blessing. I can do that. What's next?"

"Love your enemies and pray for those who despise you. It reminds me of that verse in Philippians that challenges us to not only love much, but love well."

"So love Erin and pray for her, but what about Harold?"

"I think you need to love him, too. Pray that God will enable you to love the memory of Harold, if for no other reason than Lissa's sake. And I think in learning to love him, even though he's gone, you'll be free."

Tears fell like fresh rain. "How? How do you love someone you hate?"

"Keep asking God to change your heart. You can't move forward until you go back. Someday God might bring you a new love, and I want you to be whole to receive the gift." Monica was crying, too.

"Okay." Adelaide sucked in a deep breath and wiped her tears with the sleeve of her sweatshirt, an action that would have appalled her just a few months ago.

"Forgive seventy times seven."

"That's a whole lot of forgiveness."

"Yep. Probably enough to cover both Harold and Erin, don't you think?"

Adelaide smiled. "Always the encourager."

"The great thing about God is, anything He asks us to do, with prayer and faith, He enables us to do. Next is offering the Lord a sacrifice of praise."

"Offering praise in the midst of all the hurt?"

"Yes. Not praise for the pain or necessarily the bad stuff, but praise that He is big enough to get you through, to fight your battles, to heal your hurts."

"So praise Him from my place of pain?"

"Yes, not for it, but from it."

"For the first time since Harold died, I feel hope that I can move past all this and be whole on the other side."

Monica sobbed. "I'm so glad, my friend. So glad."

Neither spoke for several minutes as they both cried with

one heart. Though separated by many miles, God bound them together in their love for Him and their friendship that carried them through laughter and tears.

Finally Monica continued, "Be kind to the ungrateful and wicked. Live beyond yourself and what you can do in your own flesh. Speak kindness and blessing to and over people—even when insulted. It's a high and hard calling." She chuckled. "Are you ready for the final warning?"

Adelaide hesitated. She was already in way over her head and far above what she could achieve. She'd have to be on her face constantly before the Lord to actually live this out. "Go ahead."

"If you succeed in living this out with the Lord, then He warns that you have to guard against pride."

Adelaide laughed. "It's always something."

"Always," Monica agreed. "Well, my friend, here is to forgiveness and freedom."

"New loves, blue skies, and God on the throne."

"Amen. Are you sticking it out then?"

"At least through the next month. I'm going to try to find a job and another place to live."

"I'm proud of you. Does this have anything to do with a certain rugged professor?"

Adelaide grinned. For the first time, he seemed like a real possibility now that she and God had started working on the Harold issues. "I'm smack-dab, head over heels in love." There, she'd said it.

❧

Isaiah had never been so relieved as when Addie's headlights lit up the driveway that evening. After searching for her high and low, he decided to come home, wait, and pray. She was ultimately in God's loving care.

Now he fought an almost overwhelming urge to run to her car, haul her into his embrace, and cover her face with his kisses. But he'd not do any of those things. He'd watch from the window as she made her way from the car to the A-frame. They had another ride scheduled on Saturday morning, so only thirty-six hours more to wait. Then he'd let her share her plans in her time and in her way. He kept begging God to convince her to stay.

Saturday morning arrived right on schedule. He'd thought long and hard about Addie the past couple of days, and one thing he knew above all else, he wanted the woman free, even more than he wanted her for himself. He wanted her free in Christ. Today he'd share his story with her. Maybe it would help.

The sun was just peeking over the horizon and the morning was chilly, but it promised to be a beautiful day. Truth be told, any day he got to spend with Adelaide proved to be a gorgeous day. Man, it had been a long time since a woman made him feel more alive just by being in the same place at the same time. He'd love to share with Addie the same deep, satisfying love he'd had with Julie. He'd been asking, seeking, knocking. Lord willing, someday the two of them might enjoy a lot more than a horseback ride together. Yep, Lord willing.

He walked past her place on his way to the barn. The windows were all closed up, so he couldn't tell if she was up yet or not. One thing he knew for certain, she was much more fragile than Julie. His pace would have to be slow and steady to win this race. No jumping in and declaring his love on date two. No sweeping Addie off her feet. So he prayed for patience every day—patience and wisdom to know how to woo her. Then for her he continually asked for freedom and healing.

After the horses finished eating, he saddled Scooter for Addie and Bart for him. And again, he found himself practicing the patience he'd been praying for. Finally, at nine he led the two horses up to her porch and knocked on the front door. She answered wearing sweats, no makeup, and a tousled head of hair. Just seeing her kicked his pulse up a notch. No doubt about it—the woman was beautiful. And he'd love to look at her day in and day out for the next hundred years or so.

"I figured under the circumstances, we should avoid each other at all cost. I just assumed our rides together would be canceled." Sincere brown eyes peered at him, fringed by thick, dark lashes.

"You're kidding, right?"

"Linda said you'd heard about the gossip." A frown drew two creases between her perfectly arched brows. From what he could tell, this woman had no flaws in her appearance. He only hoped as much for her heart someday.

"Don't assume because you might be wrong." His gaze settled on her plump, curved lips. Someday he'd claim those as his own. He could almost taste the sweetness. "Should we quit living because a few bored people have nothing more to discuss than us or the weather?"

"But—"

"No buts. Get dressed, and we'll talk about it on our ride. While you're doing that, I'll throw a lunch together. I planned on heading out hours ago, slowpoke." He smiled and glanced at his watch. "You have fifteen minutes."

He tied the horses to a pole on her porch and headed home. True to his word, he was back in fifteen minutes toting a couple of sandwiches, fruit, and Linda's famous homemade cheesecake. He knocked once, and out she came. She'd bypassed her makeup, put her hair in a ponytail, and thrown on her jeans and an old pair of Julie's boots that he'd lent her.

They rode in silence for a while—just enjoying the peace.

Finally she reined her horse to a stop, shifting in her saddle to face him. "I'm sorry." She gazed over the horizon and then refocused on him. "Seems I've brought a whole passel full of trouble your way." She smiled, but it came nowhere close to lighting her eyes. "Personally and professionally."

"When you work with college kids, nothing's a big surprise." He shrugged. "The thing is not letting it get to you."

"But the accusations Erin made tarnishes both our reputations. How do you not let it bug you? Our integrity is in question. Our names sullied."

"It will blow over."

"But that's not even the point."

"You know what I want for you?"

She shook her head. Uncertainty clouded her eyes.

"I want you to be free from others' expectations, opinions, or even accusations."

❧

Free. The same word Monica used. The same thing Adelaide longed for. Why did hearing him say it sound like criticism?

"That's my goal and dream for you—complete freedom."

Another man trying to remake me into the woman he envisions. Just like my dad. Just like Harold.

"I've lived where you are, caught up in what people think and say with regard to me. Always trying to impress and please."

Resentment flowed through her veins, and the pulse in her temple pounded.

"Julie's dad thought I could be a great guy, if I only dot, dot, dot."

Isn't that what you're doing to me at this very moment?

"The list never ended. For the first five years of our marriage, I tried to live up to his expectations, take his advice, remake myself into the guy he wanted for his daughter. Do you know where it got me?"

She shook her head. He'd seemed so different, but in truth, he was no different from any other man—controlling, demanding, dissatisfied with the way women were.

"Besides an ulcer, I was miserable, Julie was miserable, and neither of us liked the new me. Then I learned to be the man God created me to be."

"The one who hates sidewalks?" Though her tone was sarcastic, he seemed to miss it.

He smiled, and those deep dimples taunted her. "Yep. That guy. My father-in-law wanted me at some Fortune 500 company, but I'm an outdoorsman. Here is where I fit, not New York City."

"So you think I should hate sidewalks, too?"

He laughed. "No. I just want you to be the woman God created you to be."

"And you know who that is?"

Finally he caught her annoyance. "That's not what I mean at all. I just see a woman who is bound up by people rather than free in Christ. I'm sorry. I was just trying to be helpful. I didn't mean to hurt your feelings."

"How about a change of subject? I've decided to resign as your housekeeper and move—"

"Back to Dallas?" His gaze bored into her.

"I don't know. . . . Maybe." She squeezed her legs, and Scooter started up the trail again, then Adelaide glanced his direction. "I'm glad you're *free* and all"—she hadn't intended to sound so offended—"and that none of this bothers you, but I'm not so free and it really bugs me. I do care that my reputation has been tarnished."

He grabbed her rein and pulled both horses to a stop. "I do care. I hate that people are saying things about you that aren't true." He gently turned her chin with his index finger until their eyes met. His face was so near she felt his breath on her cheek. Her heart jumped into overdrive, pounding out a love song of its own. Her chin quivered in his gentle hold. Her lips dreamed of his against them. She stopped breathing as he ran his fingertips over her cheek. "I do care."

His gaze shifted to her lips. She waited, anticipating. He slipped his hand from her cheek to the back of her neck. Slowly, he pulled her toward him. Shocked at how much she wanted his kiss, she could only follow his lead. "Addie." Her name sounded like a tortured groan on his lips. "Don't leave. Not yet."

He released her and nudged his horse forward. Had she imagined the chemistry? Don't leave? *Why not?* she longed to ask, but had no idea if her voice even worked.

fifteen

Man, he'd blown it. He spent the rest of their ride quietly beating himself up. Not only had she misunderstood his freedom speech, he'd almost kissed her. What happened to patience and wisdom? Had he forgotten that she needed to heal before they moved forward? He didn't want their future intertwined with hers and Harold's past. He had to give God time to heal her.

When they stopped for lunch, they were both quiet. Finally he decided to speak up.

"I'm sorry about earlier."

She nodded, and he could see the hurt in her eyes.

"The fact is, I had no right to push my testimony on you. I just wanted you to know I've been where you are."

She shrugged. "Maybe I overreacted. I'm used to men trying to change me, and I think I took what you said a bit too personally. I've been thinking about it all morning. I know you meant well."

"So you forgive me?" He gave her a puppy-dog expression.

"With that look, how can I say no?" She smiled, and his heart lifted.

"How did your dad and Harold try to change you?" He studied her perfect complexion.

"Maybe it was more a persona they wanted from me than actually change. I don't think either cared who I actually was, as long as I presented well. For my dad, I had to be seen and not heard, respectful at all times, keep my room and appearance top-notch. Do you know he'd bounce a quarter off my bed when he inspected my room each morning? If it didn't bounce at least six inches, he'd strip my bed to the mattress and make me start again. After bed inspection came my closet. Everything had to face the same way, and each hanger was spaced two inches apart from the next one."

He listened, and his heart hurt for the little girl whose father forgot love in all his stern expectations.

"If they weren't, he took all the clothes from my closet and threw them on the floor." She threw the baggie from her sandwich into the brown paper sack. She cocked her head to the side, and a look of amazement settled over her features. "Do you know that's the first time I've told that story without pain? God is answering my prayers!" Her eyes lit up. She shared with him about her friend back in Dallas and how they'd prayed for freedom from her past.

God was answering his prayers, too. He hadn't needed his little speech from this morning. God was already taking care of things.

"I took a God-day yesterday—"

"A God-day?"

"That's what Monica and I call them. A day of fasting and being alone with the Lord. It's amazing how much healing God can do as you focus your whole self on Him through scripture reading, prayer, and praise. The irony is, I never even discussed my dad yesterday. I only asked God to heal my past with Harold and my hurts from Erin. But God went a step further! He heard my freedom cry." She bubbled in her enthusiasm.

"Do you know that I felt so much lighter at the end of the day? I still have a ways to go, but God really has begun a work. I am going to be free, Isaiah. I am. I only wish I could call Monica, but she left the country yesterday."

"I'm happy for you, and despite what you think, I'm really not trying to change you. I like you just the way you are."

"You do?" Astonishment filled her tone and expression.

"I think you're practically perfect in every way." He squeezed her hand, wanting her to believe the validity of his words.

"Me and Mary Poppins?"

"What?" He didn't follow.

"Don't you remember? She was practically perfect in every way."

"All right then, you and old Mary."

"I'm so far from perfect. I'm fearful and unforgiving. Do you know that I've held on to hurts from Harold for years and until two days ago, hadn't even realized it? Only now, after the poor man has been gone a year and a half, am I praying to love him much and love him well. Far, far from perfect."

He didn't know if now was the time, but since she was open and vulnerable, he'd ask. "What about school? Will you stay? Will you finish?"

"If I can find another job and place to live."

"Because that's what you want or because you're afraid of what people think?"

She studied him, and her brow furrowed. "I don't know. I guess because it looks bad."

"Have you met Mrs. Woods to the north of us?"

Addie shook her head.

"She's a widow. Should I move because someone might think something? Where does it end? I already feel like we've gone way over the top to guard against the appearance of evil. You don't ever come in my house if I'm home. I never come in yours. Are you happy here? Are you happy with the job?"

Adelaide searched her heart. "Honestly, I love living here. Who'd have ever thought me—Adelaide English—would love the country life?" She smiled and crossed her legs under her. "It's so. . .peaceful, and the horses. . ."

She paused and cleared her throat. "I'm sorry for making such a big deal about you raising thoroughbreds. Looking back, I sounded nuts."

"You had a deep hurt because of gambling. It's understandable that my hobby poured salt into your gaping wound. It's not only forgiven, but forgotten."

"I really am getting better, aren't I?" She shook her head. "Maybe that's why God led me here for a semester of healing. Who knows?"

"But back to my question." He leaned back on his elbow.

"I'm happy here. I adore my little A-frame, and I enjoy going to the barn every day and loving on the horses."

"You go to the barn every day?"

"You sound surprised."

"I guess I am. I didn't realize that." He looked up at the sky. "What about the job?"

"It's not my dream job, by any means, but it's not bad. Beats McDonald's."

He laughed. "Thanks. I think. What is your dream job?"

Her gaze roamed over the landscape. "I want to teach."

He grinned, obviously pleased with her choice. "Then you need to stay in school."

"I'll think about it. I will. But I don't like being pointed at or whispered about." She stood and stretched. "You ready to head back? I'm going to town later to put in some job apps."

He rose and untied his horse. "One more thing, while we're being honest. I'm sorry about earlier."

She faced him. "Earlier?"

"The near kiss." His eyes darted away.

Her face grew hot.

"It was a mistake, and it won't happen again."

Disappointment fell on her like a winter blanket. She dropped her gaze to her boots. "Okay," was her weak and pathetic response.

"So you forgive me?"

For calling the high point of her week a mistake? "No harm. No foul." Except for the little chink in her heart. For a short while she'd hoped he found her a distinct possibility, not a sizeable gaffe. Her heart felt like a yo-yo the past few days being yanked around on a string and falling from high highs to low lows.

After the ride and a shower, she got ready and headed to town. She'd decided to hit the hospital—though it had been years, she'd worked as an admittance clerk. Then she'd hit some of those adorable retail shops along the main drag. Surely she could wait on people and use a cash register. No matter what Isaiah said, she didn't feel right living in such close proximity. Right or wrong, she did care what people thought.

❧

Isaiah pulled into Walt and Linda's drive precisely at seven, surprised to see Adelaide's car in the drive.

When Walt answered Isaiah's knock and ushered him in, he heard Adelaide say, "I left home six or seven hours ago, believing I could conquer the world. Now I feel like reality conquered me, and I'll be lousy dinner company."

"What happened?" he heard Linda ask as he followed Walt around the corner and into the kitchen to join the women.

"Apparently, twenty-five years as a trophy wife does little to qualify one for a decent-paying job."

He appreciated her dry wit. He and Walt settled at the bar that divided the kitchen and dining room. Adelaide's back was to them, so she hadn't realized they were there.

"Yes, ma'am. I qualify for minimum wage fast-food-type jobs, and that's about it. The hospital doesn't care that I worked in admission twenty-some years ago. They fear the huge change in technology would leave me ill-equipped for today's needs. They no longer use a pen to fill out forms. Can you imagine that?"

Linda laughed.

"I found a tiny fixer-upper that I could afford working at the burger joint, but I fear eating may have to become optional."

Everyone laughed, and Adelaide turned to find Walt and Isaiah perched on the two bar stools. Her mouth dropped open. "Isaiah! Walt! When did you two show up and start eavesdropping on our girl talk?"

"Sorry. I just let Isaiah in, and we wandered in here. The story was so fascinating, we didn't want to interrupt."

Isaiah watched her intently and knew she didn't mind, other than being embarrassed. With Linda, she was so much more animated than with him. He'd pray for that, too. Man, his list was growing.

"Well, the bottom line is, my little nest out on Isaiah's horse farm is looking better all the time. I'm certain several mice would object to me moving into that fixer-upper. Five hundred square feet of nothing but dirt and need." She laughed, but he saw the slight droop in her shoulders.

When would she figure out that she had the best thing going? For the money, she couldn't beat it. He once again gave her to the Lord. If this was what He had for her, He'd have to convince Addie.

Linda removed a roast from the oven. "You all ready to eat?"

They settled around the little table for four. When Walt prayed, they all held hands, and his swallowed up her slender hand. This was how it should be—him covering her with safety and protection.

"I'm returning to Dallas after finals." She said it so nonchalantly as she handed him the gravy bowl.

"What?" Shock filled Linda and Walt's faces. Probably his as well.

"I can't afford to live here without the job at the school." She passed the rolls.

"What about the job at Zay's?" He was glad Linda asked the question he most wanted answered.

She shook her head. "I just don't feel right about it. Not after everything that's happened."

Walt nodded his head in understanding.

His heart sank to his knees. Wasn't anyone going to tell her how crazy that was? Apparently not, and Isaiah already had. No use beating a dead horse.

After a few minutes of silent contemplation, the mood lightened. After dinner they played cribbage. He and Addie won five out of seven games. "Well, you two make quite the pair, don't you?" Linda commented as she put the pegs away in their little slot on the bottom of the board.

I thought so.

❧

Adelaide drove herself to a different church on Sunday. She'd opted not to ride with Walt and Linda where they'd share a pew with Isaiah. She didn't want to see him any more than she had to. It was tough on the old ticker. Had she known he'd have been there last night, she'd probably have begged out on dinner as well, though she did have a great time.

And, surprisingly, no one disputed her reasons for returning to Dallas. They must agree with her that staying at Isaiah's was a bad idea. She pulled her Rodeo into an empty spot. This was a smaller church than Isaiah's, but she'd heard good things about their pastor, Franklin Jenzen. She slipped into the back row just as the worship music began.

Adelaide realized that though the adventure hadn't turned out as she planned, she was grateful for her four months in Coeur d'Alene. God had done some amazing things with her heart, and she was more whole and alive than she'd been in years. As she sang, her heart spilled over with thanks to the Lord. After the time of praise, the congregation sat down, and the pastor took the stage.

"Welcome. Today I'm teaching from the life of Benaiah on the subject of fear."

Fear? Guess God had another lesson for her to learn here in Idaho.

"Many of you may not even recognize his name, but his story is told in Second Samuel, chapter twenty-three. He was one of David's mighty men and referred to as a valiant warrior. You may turn there now if you like."

Pages turned throughout the room. Adelaide flipped there as well. "God, prepare my heart for what You have for me," she whispered, sensing this subject and sermon were no accident, but part of God's divine plan for her healing and freedom.

"Did you know that the Bible tells us to 'fear not' three hundred and sixty-five times? That is a 'fear not' for every day of the year. Faith moves God. Fear moves the enemy. Did you know that psychologists say that as of today, there are two thousand known fears and phobias? And only two are with us at birth. That's one thousand nine hundred ninety-eight learned fears. *Learned* fears.

"At birth we have the fear of falling and the fear of loud noises. That's why babies often startle easily. The other almost two thousand learned fears stop us from pursuing God's dreams."

Is that me? Adelaide squirmed in her folding chair.

"God gives us opportunities, but like Benaiah, we have to take the risk. Fear will rob us of our greatest moments. Most of our greatest moments are also some of the scariest times of our lives. Defy the odds, and ask God for the courage to pursue your own God-sized dreams. The end result is either pushing past the fear or living a life of boredom."

A life of boredom. That described what she and Harold had shared. She played it safe, never tried anything new, and life stayed uneventful. Safe and boring. Her heart pounded. Was that what she wanted? To return to safe and boring or to fight for her dream? This time she'd stay and fight. No turning tail and running back to Texas. She'd stand tall until the rumors died. And she'd even push past the fear and fight for Isaiah. With her pulse racing, she slipped out into the cold, cloudless day. God had given her a dream, and it was worth fighting for.

sixteen

"Hello?" She hadn't even glanced at the caller ID.

"Addie, it's me."

The sound of Isaiah's voice brought a shiver with it. "Hi."

"Where are you?"

"I just got out of church and was headed to the river."

"The river?"

She parked her car by Zion Hall. "I thought I'd take a walk."

"Do you mind if I join you?"

She smiled. "No, that would be fine." *Great, in fact.* "I'll meet you at your favorite spot." She kicked off her pumps and grabbed the Nikes from the seat next to her, slipping on the socks first. *I wonder what he wants.*

It was a beautiful day—even with the chill in the air. The sky was bright blue and clear. Adelaide strode across the campus and down the incline, loving the feel of the slight breeze against her face. Something about winter made her feel alive, but this year was different. She was alive, and God had lifted the cumbersome weight of bitterness from her shoulders. And today she'd stand in the face of fear and declare her plans—well, maybe not all of them. Not the ones that included Isaiah and love and maybes and someday.

Adelaide giggled. She'd never felt this giddy about a man before. Well, let's face it, there had only been one other man, and she realized they'd never experienced these "it's so great to be alive" feelings. Theirs was more of a plan—a calculated business deal. *This is what we'll do, and this is how we'll make it happen.* They cheated themselves out of so much.

Overflowing with gratitude to the Lord for second chances, Adelaide raised her eyes to the sky. "Lord, thank You. Thank You so much for the work You've started in me." She'd only had her first taste of freedom, but she wanted to enjoy it for the rest of her life. "Lord, You are good. You are good to me." She sang the chorus in a quiet voice. Her heart felt like it might explode from all the joy. And now Isaiah was joining her for her walk. Could life get any better?

She perched on top of the table and waited for him to arrive. "Lord, I'd love for him to be the one. I'd love a second chance at marriage, but a first chance at doing it right. If this is Your will for my life, turn his heart toward me."

&

There she sat, waiting for him, and what a beautiful sight she was. His heart felt light whenever she was near. How corny was that? He'd never expected to love again, so his feelings for her came as a complete surprise. He stopped and gawked, hoping she'd feel the tiniest something back, enough to make her want to stay and see where the Lord took them. Sometimes a man had to risk, and today he'd do that.

She caught a glimpse of him in her peripheral and waved. Waving back, he started down the slope. Who'd have thought that uptight woman from a few months back would now hold his heart in her hands? But she wasn't the same woman. She'd even learned to love his river. He shook his head. She'd loosened up. Yep, she'd made a lot of progress this semester, and not just academically. Adelaide English was going to be just fine. The real question was, would he if she left? Nope. He already knew the answer.

She slid from the table and took a few steps toward him.

"Is this day glorious or what?" Holding her arms out, palms raised to the sky, she spun around a couple of times.

He felt like he had a big cheesy grin plastered across his face, but he couldn't help himself.

"Let's walk." He followed her down closer to the water.

"What did you have on your mind?" she asked over her shoulder.

You. "What do you mean?"

She smiled and shook her head. "You wanted to see me, remember?"

This didn't feel like the moment to blurt it out. He'd hoped for something a bit more romantic. "I just thought we'd spend a little time together. How was church for you?"

"So good." They walked inches apart along the sandy edge. "I tried a new place this morning—the little fellowship called Christ Connection. Have you been there?"

"No. I've been at the Gathering since Julie and I first visited almost twenty-five or -six years ago."

"I really liked the pastor. Have you heard him speak? I guess he has a local radio program."

"Yeah, I've heard him a few times. He is good and solid."

"Well, today was just for me."

"Really?"

"Do you mind if we sit?"

"Not at all." Then he could watch her as she told her story. He loved the way her eyes danced when she engaged in conversation.

She glanced around and led him to a large log. They both sat. "Not extremely comfy, but better than the wet soil. Anyway, God met me in a big way today."

Her gaze locked with his. She smiled. "He's been so busy lately, I feel like I can barely keep up. So I'm hooking my seat belt and hanging on."

Isaiah loved it when anyone was excited about God, but when it was the woman he loved, all the better.

"He's been teaching me to not only forgive Harold and Erin, but to bless and love them. The coolest thing happened. Once I said okay, my heart changed toward them. The bitterness, anger, and unforgiveness evaporated, and understanding, love, and peace toward them replaced all the ugliness. Have you ever had that happen?"

"I have, and it's wonderful. Remember my father-in-law story? I know just what you are feeling."

"Why did it take me so many years? Had I only known"— her hands emphasized her words—"I could have been feeling this great all along. So today he spoke on fear. Fear. That was no coincidence."

"Nope. Providence."

"Don't you love that about God? He knew from the beginning of time that on this very day my heart would be ready to receive His message to me about fear. I find that beyond amazing."

And I find you pretty amazing yourself. She reminded him of a thirsty sponge that had been dry for years and was soaking in all the moisture it could find.

"You called me on it just yesterday, but God had you doing prep work for what He'd reveal today." She paused and took a breath. For a Texan, she could talk fast when excited. "I'm sorry, by the way, that I wasn't very receptive to what you had to say yesterday. But today, I get it—the freedom thing, the people-pleaser thing—it's all tied to fear, and do you know, I've been fearful my entire life? But not anymore. I may still feel fearful, but it's not controlling me anymore. I'm doing what God asks me to do, no matter how scary."

He wrapped his arm around her shoulder and pulled her against his side in a tight hug. "I'm so excited for you."

She leaned into him and rested her head against his shoulder. A good sign. "Me, too." A contented sigh rolled out.

❧

Something had shifted between them. Something good. He took her hand and gently rubbed her knuckles with his thumb. His touch held a promise that she couldn't explain, but she knew it was there nonetheless. This was bliss, resting in the shelter of his arms and him holding her hand. This was more than she'd hoped for. And much faster. *God, You amaze me. I stand in awe.*

"Adelaide, I don't want you to go. And I heard about this new job that might be ideal for you."

She lifted her head from his shoulder, and their eyes met. "Really? Because I don't want to leave either. Tell me about the job."

He grinned, and she settled back against his shoulder. "Bigger house, better pay. Same type of work."

"Cleaning and laundry?" Her ear against his chest picked up the steady rhythm of his heartbeat. Just like him, it was strong and dependable. "So who is it for? Anyone I know?" The new job held less appeal. Doing menial labor for someone you loved was much different from doing it for just anyone.

"Yeah, you know them. And believe me, you're much better suited for this job."

She sat up, puzzled.

He took both her hands in his and slipped from the log onto his knees in front of her. Her heart nearly floated away on a cloud. She couldn't believe this was happening. His sincere eyes looked deep into hers. They were tender and filled with love. He loved her! She saw it written all over his face. Isaiah Shepherd loved her!

"I know it's too soon, but I can't let you leave town without knowing how I feel. Addie, I'm in love with you."

Finally that kiss she'd been waiting for would come.

"I don't know exactly when or how it happened, but the thought of you leaving and me never seeing you again—well, I can't imagine anything worse."

She nodded, waiting. But her heart sang a tune all its own as his tender words flowed forth.

"I want you to be my wife. And I know this seems soon. I mean, we've never even kissed, but I think if you give me a chance, just maybe you'll grow to feel the same way I do. Will you at least stay one more semester and see where God takes us?" His voice was so earnest, so sincere.

She held her fingers up to his lips. "Wait."

His expression fell, and he started to move away from her. He'd misunderstood and thought she was rejecting his love.

"Can you go back to the part about never even kissing?" She clasped her hands behind his neck. "I think it's time we remedy that."

Joy lit his eyes. Slowly he leaned in. Her heart's pounding echoed in her ears. He stopped mere inches from her mouth. "So you want this, too?"

She didn't even bother to answer, but pulled him the rest of the way to her. And then it happened. An explosion when his lips touched hers for the first time. An explosion of heart and soul. The kiss was long—demanding, but tender.

When he raised his head, he took her face in his hands. "I love you, Adelaide English."

The words danced across her heart. She took his face in her hands and repeated his words. "And I love you, Dr. Isaiah Shepherd."

He shook his head, a look of awe on his face. "When? How did this happen?"

She laughed. "I don't know, but it did. And I've got to tell you, I thought I might die waiting for that kiss."

"Was it worth the wait?" He raised one brow.

"It was, but I won't wait that long again." And she didn't. Their second kiss was as wonderful as the first, but in it was a promise of a perfect forever for two imperfect people because in Christ was the hope and the promise.

A Letter To Our Readers

Dear Reader:

In order that we might better contribute to your reading enjoyment, we would appreciate your taking a few minutes to respond to the following questions. We welcome your comments and read each form and letter we receive. When completed, please return to the following:

Fiction Editor
Heartsong Presents
PO Box 719
Uhrichsville, Ohio 44683

1. Did you enjoy reading *Perfect Ways* by Jeri Odell?
   ❑ Very much! I would like to see more books by this author!
   ❑ Moderately. I would have enjoyed it more if

   _____

   _____

   _____

2. Are you a member of **Heartsong Presents**? ❑ Yes ❑ No
   If no, where did you purchase this book? _____

   _____

3. How would you rate, on a scale from 1 (poor) to 5 (superior), the cover design? _____

4. On a scale from 1 (poor) to 10 (superior), please rate the following elements.

____	Heroine	____	Plot
____	Hero	____	Inspirational theme
____	Setting	____	Secondary characters

5. These characters were special because? _____

_____

_____

6. How has this book inspired your life? _____

_____

_____

7. What settings would you like to see covered in future
   Heartsong Presents books? _____

_____

_____

8. What are some inspirational themes you would like to see
   treated in future books? _____

_____

_____

9. Would you be interested in reading other **Heartsong
   Presents** titles? ❏ Yes ❏ No

10. Please check your age range:
    - ❏ Under 18   ❏ 18-24
    - ❏ 25-34   ❏ 35-45
    - ❏ 46-55   ❏ Over 55

Name _____

Occupation _____

Address _____

City, State, Zip_____

E-mail _____

LOVE IS
MONUMENTAL

Heart♥ng

Any 12
Heartsong
Presents titles
for only
$27.00*

CONTEMPORARY ROMANCE IS CHEAPER BY THE DOZEN!

Buy any assortment of twelve *Heartsong Presents* titles and save 25% off the already discounted price of $2.97 each!

*plus $4.00 shipping and handling per order and sales tax where applicable.
If outside the U.S. please call
740-922-7280 for shipping charges.

HEARTSONG PRESENTS TITLES AVAILABLE NOW:

(If ordering from this page, please remember to include it with the order form.)

Presents

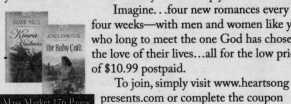